92 QUEENS ROAD

DIANNE CASE

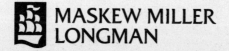

MASKEW MILLER
LONGMAN

Maskew Miller Longman (Pty) Ltd
Howard Drive, Pinelands, Cape Town

Offices in Johannesburg, Durban, King William's Town,
Pietersburg, Bloemfontein, representatives in Mafikeng
and Nelspruit and companies throughout southern and
central Africa.

website: www.mml.co.za

First published 1991
Fifth impression 2000

ISBN 0 636 01604 8

Edited by Helen Laurenson
Cover design by Lesley Sharman
Cover photographs from Cloete Breytenbach's *The Spirit of District Six*
Typeset in-house using Ventura Publisher
Imagesetting by Castle Graphics
Printed by Creda Communications, Eliot Avenue, Eppindust II, Cape Town

R9567

Dianne Case was born in Woodstock, Cape Town, in 1955. She works for a computer company and writes in her spare time. In 1980 Dianne won the ADVENTURE AFRICA AWARD with her book, *Albatross Winter*, and in 1986 her novel, *Love, David*, was the first book to win the new Maskew Miller Longman YOUNG AFRICA AWARD. Dianne is married with three daughters and lives in Lansdowne in Cape Town.

For Bonita, Maxie and Lizanne,
with love

PART I

CHAPTER 1

"Kathy! Come out of there!" Ma shouted at me.

I was sitting on Uncle Reg's leg in the back room. He had arrived that morning from Japan and, as always happened when he came back from sea, a great number of his friends had come round to see him. It was afternoon and they were telling jokes and drinking brandy and Coca Cola.

I didn't understand most of the jokes but the way they told the jokes was so funny that everyone was rolling around with laughter.

"That child has no ears!" Ma continued, shouting from the kitchen where she was shelling peas while listening to *Die Geheim van Nantes*. "... Ornaments on the sides of her head. Kathy, I spoke to you! Wait till I take my shoe off!"

Moegsien, who didn't drink alcohol because he was Moslem and it was against his religion, was telling a joke about Gammatjie and Abdoltjie in a serious, monotonous tone. Uncle Reg was sniggering and when he heard the punchline, he laughed so much that he nearly dropped me off his leg and spilled his drink on my dress.

"Kathy! I spoke to you!" Ma shouted from the doorway.

Disgustedly, she looked around the room, her eyes lingering on each of Uncle Reg's friends.

"No respect, no way to speak in front of a child," she muttered to herself, adding something to the effect that her "high blood" was "already so high!"

The sudden hush in the room indicated that the fun was over. One by one, Uncle Reg's friends rose to leave.

"Okay, Reggie," they said, "see you tomorrow."

"You ought to be ashamed of yourself, Reginald Paulse," Ma said when they had gone.

"Ag, Mommy ..." Uncle Reg said sheepishly.

"And you, young lady, go and take that dress off at once," Ma said to me.

I didn't like it when Ma was in a bad mood. She made everyone else miserable.

"Where's your mother?" Uncle Reg asked me as he helped me out of my grubby dress.

"She'll be home before *Mark Saxon and Sergei*," I said.

It wasn't long after that more of Uncle Reg's friends started arriving. They stood around awkwardly under Ma's cold glaring.

"Let's go to the Tafelberg," Uncle Reg said after a while.

I was so disappointed. I wanted him to tell me of the rough seas and how he saved the lives of his seafaring companions when the sea became treacherous. I wanted him to tell me about Japan and the people who lived there.

I guess I just wanted to be with him.

My mother came home tired and in a bad mood. She sat at the kitchen table with her ear against the transistor radio, listening to her favourite action-packed serial. Obviously lacking appetite, she moved her food around her plate with her fork.

Ma mumbled on about her high blood.

After a while, no longer able to tolerate the static, my mother licked her fork clean and stuck it into the broken bit of aerial protruding from the radio.

Thinking about Uncle Reg made me smile. He had brought me a beautiful Japanese box as a gift. It looked like a block of wood which had been highly polished and rounded at the edges, but it had many hidden compartments. It had the most wonderful pictures painted on it. On the top was a beautiful Japanese woman whose long, black hair cascaded over the exquisite turquoise and gold kimono she was wearing. An equally beautiful bird perched on her hand and she looked down lovingly at it. The rest of the box was covered with other little birds, just as pretty. I was sure they were nightingales. They were brightly coloured and life-like. I believed that if I closed my eyes and ran my fingers over them gently, I could hear them singing and see the lady smiling contentedly.

Unless you knew about it, you wouldn't find the secret panel which moved to the side, allowing the box to be opened. There were three secret compartments and it took eight moves to discover all of them.

If you shook the box, you would hear things moving about inside it. Those were all the foreign coins that Uncle Reg had put in the secret compartments for me.

CHAPTER 2

I lay in bed fondling my Japanese box and watched my mother smoking on the front stoep. It was dark and all I could see was the glow of her cigarette moving in the darkness as she periodically drew on it, but I knew it was her.

Ma sat in the kitchen listening to *Consider Your Verdict*. I knew that I would not hear Uncle Reg come home, but tried to keep my eyes open just in case.

Our house would be buzzing with activity for the next few days. Friends of Uncle Reg would come and go, as would a good number of ladies, smelling of "California Poppy". Their tiny waists would be set off by their full skirts, which would swish and swirl as they flounced about on stiletto heels, sporting fashionable marcasite jewellery.

During Uncle Reggie's stay, Ma became more bad-tempered and mumbled under her breath about her high blood pressure constantly. To underline her point, she periodically took out the white piece of cloth she kept in her breast and wiped her forehead with it.

My mother, on the other hand, seemed to enjoy the extra activity and attention. She became more friendly and approachable, but poor Cedric, our boarder, seemed to be lost and frustrated. Most nights he ended up sleeping on the couch, as Uncle Reg entertained visitors in the room that they shared until the early hours of the morning.

But once or twice, when Cedric was in the mood, he dressed up in his Connie Francis outfit and sang "Where the Boys Are" for Uncle Reg and his friends – it just depended on which friends of Uncle Reg were there. Some of his friends teased Cedric about his pink overall and high-heeled slippers and this made Cedric very cross and then he would not do anything for anyone. He would just say, "Ag, los my!" or

"You're not funny! Just leave me alone!"

"... What the neighbours must think!" Ma grumbled to my mother as she sipped her piping hot coffee on the stoep the following morning.

Ma shook her head as my mother dashed off down the road to board a bus which would take her to Salt River. There she would join the working class, bent over a sewing machine in a clothing factory until five o'clock.

Mrs Abrahams, Radia's mother, was already sweeping her stoep. I wondered if Radia was awake yet, because I wanted to show her my Japanese box. Mrs Abrahams called out a cheery, "Good morning, Mrs Paulse!" to Ma. "I see Reggie's home," she continued as she descended the steps and walked onto the pavement and began sweeping there too.

"Yes," Ma replied curtly, in no mood to strike up a conversation, and fussed about with her pot plants on the wrought iron stand against the wall.

"Will he be home for long?" Mrs Abrahams persisted.

"Go and get dressed!" Ma snapped at me, pretending not to hear Mrs Abrahams. She walked into the house, the floorboards creaking under her considerable weight.

"Who does that woman think she is?" Ma mumbled as she opened the kitchen window, "... to question me like that! Is it any of her business?"

"Ma, can I have my Mommy's coffee?" I asked.

"No!" she said irritably. "It's unhealthy for children to drink such hot coffee so early in the morning!"

I couldn't wait for Uncle Reg to get up in the mornings, and many times I would tip-toe to the door of the back room and listen to his snoring. I would drop things on the floor loudly and make loud, noisy sounds in the hope of waking him.

"Get away from that door – at once!" Ma shouted at me now.

Ma went through her household chores and I did what I usually did, fetching the letters from the postman, rinsing the milk bottles and putting them on the stoep for the milkman for the next morning, and emptying the cold tea left in the teapot onto the plants.

Eventually Uncle Reg rose and came into the kitchen – yawning, stretching, barefoot and clad in nothing but his underpants.

"Where's your self-respect?" Ma snapped at him. "You could at least get dressed!"

Uncle Reggie paid no attention to her. He pretended that I was a weight as I hung onto his forearm and, holding his breath as he did when he actually picked up his weights – which he claimed made all the young ladies go crazy – he hoisted me up and down.

"There's hot water," Ma said.

"Good," he said, and went out into the yard to fetch a basin to wash himself in.

He joked as he poured the hot water into the basin, pretending that the splashes which caught his bare chest were causing him much pain.

"Aah! Aah! Aah!" he went, pulling funny faces which had me in a fit of giggles.

He glanced through the old newspapers which he spread on the floor and table to catch the splashes that flew around as he washed himself. He hummed and whistled as he vigorously soaped himself, not even taking care to keep the soap from his eyes.

"Kathy, come away from there!" Ma demanded. "Little girls must not watch big men when they wash themselves!"

I followed her into the back room.

"This room stinks!" she said as she drew back the curtains and opened the windows.

CHAPTER 3

As I had anticipated, the following few days were blissful. Uncle Reg was big and strong and such fun. He gave me money every day and said:

"Go and buy us something nice at Motjie Ismail's shop on the corner."

"Nice like what, Uncle Reg?" I asked him.

He closed one eye and looked up with the other as if thinking hard.

"How about some canned peaches and Nestlé's cream, or a family block?" he said.

"I am warning you, Reggie," Ma said, "you are spoiling that child."

Uncle Reg spoiled all of us, even Ma.

In the afternoons he sat on his bed in the back room, his back resting against the wall and his shirt unbuttoned, strumming his guitar. He knew only one chord, although he positioned his fingertips on the strings like a professional, and since he did not sing anything else, only one line of a song:

"Tell me, Dear – are you lonesome – tonight?"

On the odd evening he sat on the stoep with my mother and played the same tune with such expert confidence, especially if some young ladies were walking past, that you would think he had composed the words and the melody himself.

And then it was time for him to sail the perilous seas again.

It was a Sunday and as usual, we had all the family to lunch, but is was more unpleasant than pleasant because my Aunty Marjorie's sister (who had left her husband) and her three children also came along, and they made the house feel so full.

My mother's eldest brother, my Uncle Peter, was Aunty Marjorie's husband, and they had two sons – Edward and Christopher.

My mother was the youngest and Uncle Reg was the second child. My cousins were both older than I was and spoke about school and bioscope and things that I had no experience of, but today they ignored me, because their other cousins were there and together they teased me no end.

My two uncles stood on the stoep admiring uncle Peter's car. It was a beautiful vehicle – black and shining. When no-one was looking, I dared to sneak up to it and touch it, while peering inside.

My cousins ran up and down the passage, making a terrible noise and knocking the ornaments off the dresser. My aunt and her sister helped in the kitchen by peeling vegetables and making tea. They expressed their sympathies for Ma's blood pressure problem.

My mother seemed to be as left out of things as I was.

Uncle Reg was trying to pack in the back room, but my cousins kept disturbing him, and also, his friends kept coming to say good-bye.

The smell of roast potatoes wafted through the house, as did the musical strains from *The Bell Tower*, accompanied by the shrill singing of my aunt and her sister: "How great Thou art!"

Eventually Uncle Reg sent all us children to Motjie Ismail to buy suckers. "Kathy will take you," he said, smiling at me kindly and giving me a ten shilling note.

Aunty Marjorie complained that Uncle Reg was spoiling the children again and that we should first eat our food before being given luxuries.

"I don't believe in giving children luxuries," her sister said. "That is why they get such a lot of rotten teeth and when they must get them pulled out, they want to scream and perform!"

"That's Reggie for you," Ma said. "You can count on him to spoil the children."

"Then when they grow up they have no respect," Aunty Marjorie continued.

"Ag, man, they're only kids," Uncle Reg said, and urged me to go.

Lunch was rushed and staggered since there were not enough plates. After lunch Uncle Peter started conveying everyone, trip by trip, to the docks to see Uncle Reg off.

My mother and I were the last to leave the house and soon it was evening already and all the visitors were ashore and the tug was leading the ship away from the quay. The sun cast orange ripples across the sea as the boat sounded its horn. Uncle Reg saw me. He waved to me and I waved back and then he blew his love to me in a kiss. Uncle Peter was saying that we must go back and Ma said her feet were killing her.

The water was churning frothy and white as the ship moved out to the greater ocean.

Uncle Reg was truly on his way.

* * *

We were all crammed into the car. Ma sat in front with me on her lap. My older cousins did not like this idea, and nudged one another.

Aunty Marjorie squealed that someone had hurt her foot.

I kept my eyes on the fading shadow of the ship in the darkening distance. I wanted to see it cross the line which was the horizon.

When we reached our house we looked out at the sea from the stoep. My cousins said that they could see the ship and I said I could see it too.

"Wê-la!" they shouted at me together. "You can't see anything! It's too dark! You always think you are great and know everything, but you know nothing!"

"Uncle Reggie's on the other side of the world already," my cousin Edward said.

"Oh no, he's not!" I argued. "He told me it would be a lot of days before he is on the other side of the world and he is going to bring me a present from Spain – he's not going to bring any of you anything because you are all too rude!"

"You believe everything Uncle Reggie says because you are stupid and you are a girl," they teased.

"And your Uncle Reggie isn't even her father," their aunt's youngest daughter said.

I felt the tears brimming in my eyes.

"She hasn't even got a father," Christopher, my eldest cousin, said.

"Ma!" I cried, running into the house.

"Edward and Christopher!" their mother shouted at them when she heard what they had said about me.

"Tell them sticks and stones will break your bones, but names will never hurt you," Uncle Peter said, and added with a laugh: "Boys will be boys."

I crept into the front bedroom which my mother and I shared with Ma and hid underneath Ma's double bed, waiting until I could be quite sure that they had all left.

The floor vibrated as they ran up and down the passage, sliding on the blue linoleum. I was not going to come out of hiding until I was sure that they had gone, not even if someone called me. The sounds of washing-up in the kitchen slowly lulled me to sleep.

CHAPTER 4

Things were very much quieter, but pretty much back to normal the following day. I spent much of the morning on the stoep, from where I had an uninterrupted view of the harbour. Far beyond the cranes and the late.March misty haze, I knew that somewhere on that very sea, the *SA Vaal* sailed forth with Uncle Reg aboard, playing the part he had to play in order for the ship to accomplish her mission. I felt that as long as I could see the sea, Uncle Reg would be close to me.

Luckily, our house was on the right side of the road to afford us this beautiful view. On the other hand, the houses on the other side of the road had a full view of Table Mountain in all her majesty – the view which we had from the back room window.

Our house was one of a row of terraced houses which Ma claimed had been built long before the War. That was something about Ma that never failed to amaze me. Whenever she spoke in terms of time, all that mattered to her was whether it was before the War or after the War.

Each house had a long passage, off which were the rooms. The main bedroom was first, then the sitting room, the kitchen and the back room, in that order. The floors were wooden, hollow and highly polished, and creaked when you walked down the passage. They also had intermittent holes through which many a coin had fallen.

Apart from the sitting room, each room had a sash window. The walls were stippled and painted egg-yellow apart from the back room and kitchen, which were painted a yellowish-green. If I ran my hand over the green walls, a powdery residue would come off onto my hand.

The ceilings were high and painted white. They were also wooden. In the summer they were dotted with flies in spite of the flycatchers which hung suspended from them – yellow at first, and then crusty and black as the flies became trapped in their stickiness.

It was a big fuss, hanging flycatchers. Ma would call on Thomas, a big boy who lived further down the road. He would have to balance on a rickety chair which was placed on the kitchen table and, squinting his eyes and using all the strength he could muster, he would have to press the drawing pin into the wooden ceiling, taking care not to get the sticky, gluey flycatcher in his hair.

Removing the thing from the ceiling was quite simple. Ma would simply grab at it with a newspaper and bundle it all up.

The yard was small and cemented, with an afdakkie under which we hung our washing when it rained. The lavatory was also in the yard. It was a modern one with a chain that flushed the bowl when you pulled it. The back gate which opened into the lane behind the houses was old, wooden and broken. It was pushed closed and kept so by two bricks pushed hard against it.

Living in the yard was Spotty – our fat Fox Terrier dog with a curly tail, which one of Cedric's clients at the hairdresser had given him once. Ma said Spotty was a stupid dog because he never ever caught a burglar, but Cedric said he would – one day – when a burglar called at our house. Spotty slept in a box under the afdakkie and was not allowed in the house.

Then, of course, there were the smells and the sounds that made this house our home: the eerie creaking of the floors and the doors; the dripping brass tap in the kitchen, which continued to drip, drip, drip in spite of being fitted with countless new washers by Mr Jansen, an old man who did odd jobs in the neighbourhood for a packet of cigarettes; and the cooing of Mr Petersen's racing pigeons in the yard next door to ours.

There were the Friday smells of polish, brass cleaner and fish frying in hot oil, and the smell of Brylcream in the back room and bread-baking on Sunday mornings, and yes, the wonderful smell of the sea when the north wind blew, heralding the approach of rain.

CHAPTER 5

During Uncle Reg's absence I spent a lot of time with Radia and her brother, Fadiel, from next door. Their grandmother or Oemie, as we called her, lived in Salt River and made the most exquisite wedding dresses. Often the brides would need a pretty girl for their flower-girl and Oemie would offer Radia, so Radia had a range of the most breathtakingly beautiful flower-girl dresses in the most delicate pastel shades, made of chiffon, lace and tulle and trimmed with diamantés, pearls and sequins. Often, if her mother was in a good mood, she would allow us to put the dresses on, especially if her sister, Aunty Mariam, was there with her daughter, Sumaya.

We would twirl and swish and pretend that the tiaras on our heads were crowns and that we were princesses – the daughters of a jealous king who kept us locked up because he did not want the men of his kingdom to see us. We would lament that we would never marry if we did not meet any suitors.

Sometimes, when it was raining on a Sunday and my cousins Edward and Christopher came for lunch, Radia and Fadiel would come over and we would play "Blind Man's Bluff" in the back room until Ma complained of the noise. During the summertime, the boys caught bees which they kept in peanut-butter jars, while Radia and I made daisychains, which we put in our hair and around our necks.

One day Radia and I were playing "Si-Boom, Si-Boom" in the road just before lunch.

We jumped across three squares of nine squares which we drew in the road with a piece of brick, which we found on the field at the back of the houses.

Our hair and our skirts twirled and fluttered around us in the gentle April wind as we jumped across in precise rhythm in opposite directions to each other, and then changed position and jumped the other way, all the time saying, "Si-boom si-boom, si-boom si-bay, boom-bay … "

Radia stopped to tuck her dress into her bloomers.

"There's your mother," she said, pointing down the road.

"At work, of course," I gasped, quite out of breath.

"Not where – there," she said.

It was my mother coming up the road – I recognised her clothes and bag. Her long hair glided behind her as the wind gathered momentum and picked it up.

I didn't know whether I should run and tell Ma or whether I should run and meet my mother, but Radia decided that for me. She bounded off down the road, me after her, and fell into step next to my mother, proudly taking her bag from her.

All the neighbours who were out sweeping their stoeps or outside their gates stopped to greet her. She smiled and greeted each one by name, not stopping to talk as most would have liked. As soon as we passed them, they would look at one another, speculating on her coming home from work so early.

The call of the man in the mosque rose above the wind.

"I must go now," Radia said, "there's the belal."

Ma was cross. She demanded to know why my mother was home so early and then stopped to tell me to go outside and not to mind "big people's" business.

I went to play in the back room, from where I could hear everything.

My mother sat down at the kitchen table and kicked her shoes off, while Ma put water on for tea.

"I lost my temper with the supervisor," my mother began explaining.

"But you need the job," Ma interrupted.

"There's just so much you can take," my mother argued.

"Did you get your unemployment card?" Ma asked.

My mother fumbled in her bag and produced a khaki-coloured card.

"They put a one on it," she said.

"Why didn't you report her to the manager?" Ma asked.

"What's the point?" my mother asked. "They are as thick as thieves – always covering for each other."

"I suppose you can sign for unemployment," Ma said after a brief silence.

"I'll get a job," my mother said. "There are lots of places opening up. *They* are not my beginning and my end."

Ma began telling of when Aunty Baby, her youngest sister, who had died many years before I was born, was a young apprentice to a dress shop and how badly the other girls treated her because they were jealous of her.

" ... because she was very pretty," Ma said, "but she stuck it out and look how far she came," she concluded.

"There are lots of small places opening up and looking for machinists," my mother said.

"They are all immigrants," Ma said thoughtfully. "You don't know if you can trust them."

"As long as they pay, I don't care what they are," my mother said.

There was another pause as Ma poured the boiling water onto the leaves in the aluminium teapot.

"You should go back tomorrow and apologise," Ma said, looking into the teapot as if she expected the very tea leaves to get up and give her moral support.

"I'm finished with them," my mother said firmly.

"You've always been too cheeky for your own good," Ma said.

"Don't worry," my mother said quietly now, "I'll get another job tomorrow."

"I hope you're right," Ma said, pouring the tea into the cups, "Because I can't support you!"

The two of them sat opposite each other at the kitchen table, avoiding each other's eyes. Simultaneously, they stirred the sugar into their tea – Ma beating hers and my mother stirring hers with decided determination. Silently, the two of them drank the hot brew.

The clock ticked diligently on the mantlepiece in the

sitting room, its tick-ticking reaching the kitchen and the back room. The washing fluttered about on the line in the backyard as the wind picked up and a wall of cloud came cascading over the mountain.

"The weather's changing," Ma said, as she replaced her cup on her saucer with a clink.

CHAPTER 6

That evening, two women from my mother's work came to visit. They discussed how unfair the supervisor had been, how she passed all the most unpleasant tasks onto my mother, and how my mother got the blame for the wrongdoings of others.

"She did the right thing to walk out," the one woman said.

Ma seemed to know better.

"Is she Malay?" Ma asked.

The woman nodded.

"I thought so," Ma said smugly.

My mother shook her head in disgust.

"You don't want to listen," Ma said. "You don't find them any different, always standing up for each other."

The women left, each promising to find out about work for my mother from some relative or other.

Over supper, Ma told my mother of all the chores she wanted her to help with the following day – things like cleaning the windows and putting fresh paper in the drawers.

But that was not to be.

It was still dark and we were all sleeping when Cedric came to knock on our bedroom door.

"Hier's ene vir Bertha," he said, still rapping at the door.

"What's it, Cedric?" my mother asked, most agitated.

"Someone to see you, Bertha," he said.

I jumped out of bed and made for the front door. Cedric mumbled and went back to the kitchen, where he fumbled with the tea things.

There was a man in a white coat standing on the stoep, facing the road, where a taxi stood, engine still running.

"Waar's jou Ma?" he asked me irritably.

"I'm here, I'm here," she answered behind me, stuffing her feet into Ma's slippers.

She seemed to know the man, as she greeted him by name. They spoke on the stoep for a short while and he handed her a piece of paper.

"Do you want coffee?" she asked.

"Ek's haastig," the man said, and left, his big black taxi leaving a trail of smoke behind him.

"What is it?" Ma asked, awake now.

"It's a job," my mother said.

"Where?"

"Long Street."

"Must be a Jew," Ma said thoughtfully.

"As long as the money's okay, I don't care what they are," my mother said.

"Mmm," Ma said.

It was too early to get up, but it was too late to fall asleep again. We lay there, the three of us, listening to the sounds of the morning.

Cedric was still busy in the kitchen, knocking cups on saucers, dropping a teaspoon to the floor, stirring the leaves in the teapot, his feet shifting to and fro.

Spotty, hearing activity in the kitchen, began yapping at the back door for a tit-bit.

Ma began telling my mother how she used to work "in service" long before she met Pa, my grandfather, and they were married. Pa died long before I was born.

"That was the only work we could get in those days," she said.

Then she told us again about Aunty Baby and how pretty she had been and what a beautiful voice she had had.

"She used to sing: 'I will take you home, Kathleen …' " And Ma would sing the old song for us in her shrill voice.

"So many men fell in love with her," Ma mused.

" … To where your heart will feel no pain … " Ma sang.

"Yes, she was beautiful," Ma sighed. "She looked like a goddess."

"What happened to her, Ma?" I asked, prompting Ma, even though I had heard the story before.

"What happened to her?" Ma repeated. "She fell in love with the wrong man and died of a broken heart."

She was quiet for a while, lost somewhere in the memories of her beautiful sister.

After a while she began to sing again – this time softer, as if to herself only:

"… to where the grass is always green … "

The early buses passed along the Main Road below and the man in the mosque cleared his throat and began to sing out, heralding the time for Moslem people to rise for the first prayer of the day.

"Wil Antie Lenie tee hê?" Cedric asked, tapping softly on the slightly ajar bedroom door.

"Please, Cedric," my mother answered.

Cedric said, "Tch," but he brought two cups of tea anyway.

"It's going to be a nice day," he said.

I jumped over to my mother's bed under the window and parted the curtains.

Nurse, with her case at the back of her bicycle, was returning exhausted in her white uniform from having delivered a baby.

The milkman was running up the road, his bottles clinking.

There was a grey mist over the sea – no sign of the sun yet, but day was breaking over the tops of the cranes which peeked out eerily above the mist, while everything enveloped in it seemed to be asleep.

"Uncle Reg is still sleeping," I said.

"Yes, Kathy," my mother, said tickling me on my side with her long nails.

I rolled over in a fit of laughter, almost knocking the cup of tea over.

"Bladdy stupid!" Ma said. "You could have burnt the child!"

"I was just playing with her," my mother said sheepishly.

CHAPTER 7

I watched my mother as she put on a dress and took it off again; then she tried on something else and took that off again. Soon she was trying on Ma's clothes. Finally she settled for the outfit she had tried on first. She had some very beautiful clothes.

She had the same problems with her shoes.

She put on her lipstick and then took the silver wavers out of her hair.

"You look nice," I said, when she finally left.

"As long as she can do the work, he's not going to look at her," Ma said as we saw her on her way.

My mother said she could walk to Long Street – "but not for the interview and not in these high heels" – so she would take the bus.

"She'll probably start today," Ma said.

I played on the stoep after breakfast, expecting to see my mother returning from the interview.

Nurse, on the other side of the road, called me to go to the shop for her.

"First ask your Ma," she said.

Ma said, "That woman is just too lazy for words, but go maar."

Nurse gave me a shilling to buy a bottle of paraffin and a sucker for myself.

The shop wasn't far and I liked going to Motjie Ismail, especially if Baai was there. He always gave me a bubblegum, which I had to hide from Ma, because she said that bubblegum was made of elephants' snot and that it could choke you, but Baai said it wasn't. Anyway, carefully carrying the empty bottle under my arm, I trotted off to the shop.

"Kathy! I've got something for you!" Baai said excitedly.

He served all the other people first, then he took me to the stoep at the back where the paraffin and fish oil were kept in the big drums. He filled my bottle with paraffin and took me back inside the shop.

He fumbled about in a jar and then he said:

"Open your hands and close your eyes."

I did as he said, holding my breath and enjoying the excitement that rippled all over me.

"Open sesame!" he said, placing something in my hand.

Filling the palm of my hand was a beautiful gold coin. It was so beautiful, it took my breath away.

"Is this for me?" I asked. "To keep?"

"Yes, Gogga," he said. "It's our new money. That's a cent!"

"Oh!" I said.

"We are not going to have pennies any more," Baai explained.

"I must show my Ma," I said.

Outside the shop I put the bottle of paraffin down and looked at the coin again.

It had an ox-wagon on it which seemed to be so right, although I didn't know why. It glinted in the sunshine with almost blinding flashes of light.

"It's beautiful," I whispered to myself.

It felt as if I had captured a handful of golden sunshine as I held it to my chest – the most precious thing. All along the way home, I put the bottle of paraffin down and examined the coin again, fingering the impressions on it.

I showed Nurse the coin, but she was not impressed. All she wanted was her change, which I had left at the shop in my excitement.

"You'll have to go back for it," she said.

"I'll have to first ask my Ma!" I replied, and ran home.

CHAPTER 8

Ma frowned at the coin.

"I don't know about rands and cents," she said. "I don't think I'll ever understand them. No more twelve pennies in a shilling – only ten. Then what happened to the other two?"

"Yoo-hoo!" Nurse called from the gate.

Ma waddled down the passage, her swollen slippered feet shuffling over the shiny linoleum.

"Het Nurse die nuwe geld gesien?" Ma asked her.

"I saw it, I don't like it, there is going to be a lot of confusion, but who will listen to me? My change, please, Kathy!" she said all in one long, monotonous breath.

"Oh, yes," I said, and jumped over the wall to go to the shop.

"Kathy!" Ma said, and Nurse shook her head.

"I'm so tired," she told Ma "… up all night!"

There were lots of people in the shop – all complaining about, "What happens to the other two pennies?"

"The Government will claim it!" an irate old man shouted hysterically. "They'll take everything away from us – just you mark my words!"

"People, people," Mr Ismail's son, Dullah, said. "It had to happen. It is part of an independence. We are no longer the Colony of South Africa – we are the Republic of South Africa and the rands and cents are our very own money. The pennies and shillings belong to Britain!"

"Two pennies is two pennies," someone said.

"Yes, it's not two ha'pennies or two farthings," someone else added.

"There's a lot you can do with two pennies," someone else said.

"It's decimal money," someone said. "Decimal Dan,

remember?"

"Look," Dullah was saying, "we don't fall under Britain any more – we are out of the Commonwealth."

I wormed my way through the crowd and, standing on my toes, tapped on the counter.

Baai saw me and handed me the change, which was wrapped up in a bit of newspaper.

"You forgot this, sweetheart," he said.

I wormed my way back through the crowd.

"We are a country on our own now," Dullah was saying, his young wife standing nervously at his side with their young child on her hip.

"We don't answer to Britain any more, or any other country, for that matter."

I trotted home, trying to understand the confusion of the people at the shop. I kept thinking of what Dullah said – that we were standing on our own as a country.

I was only six years old and I didn't quite understand what a country was except that it was the far-away places where Uncle Reg went with his ship. Well, we lived in a place, so it had to be a country too. Suddenly it all made sense.

Nurse was still standing at the gate, her straggly long hair hanging limply over her white uniform.

"… No offence to Kathy," she said, "but I don't deliver babies to unmarried mothers. No, sir, I don't like to dirty my hands, and if it wasn't that our minister asked me, I would have said 'No'!"

She took the money from me and put it in her pocket.

I heard what Nurse said, but didn't understand what she meant, although I remembered it for a long time.

CHAPTER 9

My mother returned home in a very jolly mood. "There was no interview," she said, kicking off her shoes. "I just started working. Mummy, you will laugh. He takes me up to here," she said, indicating her shoulders. "There's another girl, Dolores, just the two of us. The boss, I've forgotten his name, but Dolores calls him 'Rab', makes the tea and sweeps the floors. He's old, shame, and he sits on boxes – Mummy, he doesn't even have a chair and he never changes the expression on his face. Dolores and I laughed all day."

"I told you to expect to start," Ma said. "What do you people make and how's the machines?"

"Shirts," she said, throwing her head back and laughing. "We make shirts, shirts and more shirts – we do everything ourselves, cutting, stitching, to sewing on the buttons. Old Rab makes the patterns himself, but he's so slow!"

"Is he in the Union?" Ma asked.

"I don't think so. Mind you, Dolores says he pays more than the Union rates."

Do you know, my mother was so excited that she missed half of *Mark Saxon and Sergei*? All she could speak about was Rab and Dolores.

Ma was pessimistic.

"No Union," she said thoughtfully. "What if you hurt yourself? I don't know about such small places."

"Dolores says he's okay. She's been with him for two months already."

"That doesn't mean a thing," Ma said.

My mother's personality was transformed overnight. She was happy to get up in the mornings and came home in a good mood. Sometimes she came home later and said that she and Dolores had walked all the way.

"It's not far," she said cheerfully.

Every night she gaily related some of her and Dolores's antics with Rab. Then one Thursday she announced that Dolores was coming home with her the following night and was going to spend the weekend.

"How could you invite her?" Ma hissed. "You know there's no place for her."

"She sort of invited herself, you know."

"I don't know," Ma said. Then she added as an afterthought, "Mind you, Marjorie left a message with Nurse that they won't be coming through on Sunday, so I suppose it's all right."

Dolores had an infectious personality. She had no inhibitions, no airs and graces. She crept into everyone's heart and stayed there. Even Ma took to her, although she didn't say so. Dolores became like a child in our house. She was petite and pretty with flashing green eyes. Soon she was spending nearly every weekend at our house, she and my mother sharing Uncle Reg's bed in the back room. She insisted that Cedric still sleep in his bed and always included him in their discussions and jokes. Since he was a hairdresser, she persuaded him to cut and set her hair every Saturday afternoon. Normally, Cedric didn't do that for anyone on a Saturday because it was his busiest day. What with weddings and functions, he worked from early in the morning to quite late most times, but he didn't mind attending to Dolores, sometimes even looking for her so that he could "do" her hair. In return, Dolores helped Cedric to wash all the towels from the hairdresser, sometimes getting my mother involved as well, even though she complained about it.

It was easy to understand how my mother had become enchanted with her.

Dolores told us that her mother lived in Johannesburg and that they were not in touch. She had been reared by her granny's friends and boarded with them in Constitution Street.

She put her hand to cleaning the house too, packing and

unpacking cupboards, putting fresh newspaper into drawers, and encouraging Ma and my mother to throw out all the useless old junk that cluttered the place.

She washed my hair and dressed me up, lipstick and all, for walks to Town on Sunday afternoons to window-shop.

She liked Elvis and danced with vibrant energy. She said things like "See you later, Alligator," to which we had to reply, "In a while, Crocodile," and then her face would crease with amusement and she'd giggle – delicious, infectious laughter that had everyone else giggling too.

CHAPTER 10

Radia was looking forward to the month of Ramadan or fasting. Her parents had decided that this year, since she was seven years old and at school, she would fast half days and that Fadiel, who was ten, would fast full days. When the time came, Radia coped well, but poor Fadiel had a hard time. His lips were chapped and he had a headache every day. Their mother told Ma that it was like that the first time, but that he would get used to it.

Every evening just before Magrieb – the evening prayer which indicated the setting of the sun and the end of the day's fasting – little Moslem girls, white scarves on their heads, were busily running errands in the neighbourhood. They carried plates of koeksisters, dhaltjies or samoosas, covered with drying-up cloths, and these they proudly distributed to various neighbours.

Radia always brought us something nice and half-way through the fast, when they ate boeber, she brought us a jug of that too.

Then there was Labarang – the celebration at the end of the month's fasting. Fadiel and his father gathered with the other men on Signal Hill the night before to confirm the sighting of the new moon, which was the sign that the month had ended.

Little Moslem children were dressed in their new clothes and new shoes. The girls had colourful dresses, bobby socks and patent leather shoes. They carried bags to match their shoes and walked in groups from door to door to say "Slamat" to other Moslem people in the area, who would give them a few coins to carry in their bags.

"I wish I was Moslem," I said to Ma as we watched the children from the stoep.

"Don't talk nonsense!" Ma snapped at me irritably.

Eventually Guy Fawkes day arrived, accompanied by great excitement in the neighbourhood.

The bigger children gathered on the field behind the row of houses and made a "Guy". They stuffed a discarded old suit that had belonged to some man with balls of rolled-up newspaper. They stuffed a nylon stocking with newspapers too and fitted this to the neck of the suit to make a head. They put an old hat on top of the head and forced the bulging ends of the trousers into an old pair of shoes.

The "Guy" was now complete and was lifted very carefully into an old baby's push-cart.

The "Guy" was pushed down the street with all the children running after it, singing, "Guy het nie hare nie, Guy het nie hare nie!" The older children knocked on the doors and demanded:

"Penny for the Guy, penny for the Guy!"

I stood back to watch them knock on Nurse's door and collapsed in a heap of laughter when they did.

"Shoo! Get away from here!" Nurse scolded them. "Go on! I haven't got time for silliness!"

By late afternoon they had collected quite a mound of cents and half-cents and had bought fire-crackers – lots of big bangs, which made a terrific noise, and sky rockets, which soared into the night sky in a trail of light.

Poor Spotty didn't know what was going on. He was terrified and howled and scratched at the back door, but Ma would not let him in.

We all stood on the stoep watching the activity in the neighbourhood. Dolores and Cedric were there too.

The two of them had become quite fond of each other. They practised all the latest dance steps together and gossiped about the people Cedric worked with.

They often went out together at weekends to dances or the bioscope. "So that we have someone to dance with," Dolores would argue with my mother when she objected to having Cedric with them.

Dolores defended Cedric when people made fun of him.

"He can't help it," she would say. "He is also someone's child."

My mother was getting tired of Dolores, though. She often gossiped to Ma about her.

"She stays away from work for any little thing," she would say. "Cramps, a headache … and the number of funerals she goes to is nobody's business – I'm sure she doesn't know half the people!"

"Maybe she only says she is going to a funeral," Ma said thoughtfully.

"That's also true," my mother said.

Dolores was not aware that she was losing popularity. She had heard that Uncle Reg was coming home soon and seemed set on meeting him. I wondered what he would think of her.

CHAPTER 11

Uncle Reg duly arrived with his assortment of friends, and Ma's high blood shot up immediately.

"I'm not taking it!" she said defiantly.

Uncle Reg, somewhat under the weather, said "Shh!" to Ma and held his forefinger to his lips.

Ma wiped her forehead with her apron. Cedric told Ma to sit down and put on water for tea. Meanwhile, Uncle Reg and Dolores were stealing glances at each other.

"She isn't even shy," my mother complained to Ma afterwards.

Uncle Reg had brought me the most beautiful Spanish doll with a magnificent, frilly, red dress. She had long, plaited black hair which hung over her breast down to her waist, and she wore a black hat with tassels around the brim.

She had a miniature guitar on a strap over her shoulder. Her dainty little fingers were placed on the strings as if she were playing. She was dazzlingly beautiful. I was scared to touch her in case I should spoil her.

"Her name's Lola," Uncle Reg said.

"You must keep her in the box so that you can show your children one day," Ma said.

"You should have brought her something she could play with," Dolores said to Uncle Reg, who winked at her.

The following day I helped Uncle Reg sort out the clothes in his suitcases. We smelt everything and said "Clean," or "Dirty," and dropped the clothes into separate piles.

Uncle Reg gave me all the foreign coins which he found in his pockets.

"I almost forgot something," I said, jumping up.

I ran to ask Ma for the cigar box with all my coins, which was kept in her wardrobe. She was irritable, but I kept on and eventually she gave it to me, scolding that whenever Uncle Reg was home, I became "out of hand".

I threw all the coins out onto Uncle Reg's bed.

"Open your hands and close your eyes," I said to him.

Amused, he did as I said and I placed the one cent coin in his hand.

"Now open," I said.

He examined the coin, muttering that he had seen it before.

"Aren't you proud of our country and our new money, Uncle Reg?" I asked.

"Darling, Darling," he said, "This is not our country. We have no say here. We don't belong here. This is not our country."

I frowned at him for a while. I was looking for a sign that he was teasing me. He carried on packing his clean clothes into the wardrobe and throwing the dirty things on the mat.

With a sigh I dropped my coins into the cigar box, one by one listening for the clinking sound of metal falling on metal. I kept my one cent coin in my left hand, all the while fingering it.

I wondered if Uncle Reg understood the enormity of what he had just said. I looked at him, but his eyes would not meet mine as he busily sorted his socks into soiled and unsoiled heaps. I wondered if he had changed in the months he had been away.

His words kept echoing round and round in my head, words that made me feel sad although they were spoken with such tenderness.

"This is not our country … We don't belong here!"

I was born in this very house, so was he. How could he say we didn't belong here?

"Uncle Reg", I said softly, "where do we belong?"

He picked me up and put me on top of his wardrobe, my legs dangling down. He looked me in the eye and tapped the tip of my nose.

"You're too young to worry about that!" he said.

CHAPTER 12

Radia liked Lola, but she was more excited about her own news.

"First toss in because it's a secret," she said.

We hooked our pinkies together, so pledging absolute trust in each other.

She looked at me with mischief and magic in her eyes and sighed.

"What is it?" I asked impatiently.

"I'm not supposed to tell," she said, drawing in a deep breath.

"You must tell," I persuaded her. "We tossed in!"

"But you can't tell anyone," she said, "not even your Mommy, not even your Ma, not even Uncle Reggie … "

"I won't tell, Radia," I said. "We tossed in, remember?"

Painstakingly, she moved my hair behind my ear and then cupped her hand over it and whispered something so fast, I didn't hear it.

"What?" I asked.

"My mommy's going to buy us a baby – a girl, I think, so I will have a sister *and* a brother to play with!"

Pangs of jealousy jabbed at me. Why couldn't my mother buy that little girl baby so I could have a sister? Radia already had a brother. If I had a little sister to play with, Ma wouldn't have to keep telling me to keep out of big people's company. I would push my baby sister up and down the road in her pram and I'd brush her hair and wipe her nose. Radia had everything. She had a father, she had a brother, she had beautiful flower-girl dresses and shoes and now she was going to get a brand new baby sister. It wasn't fair.

"I don't feel like playing any more," I said, and placed Lola back in her box.

"Why?" Radia asked.

"Because when you have your baby sister, you won't play with me any more!"

"Of course I will," she argued. "We are best friends!"

"But when you have a sister you will forget you have a best friend."

"I won't," she pleaded, and added quickly. "I'll let you also play with my baby sister!"

"Can I push her in her pram?" I asked.

Radia nodded, the magic in her eyes replaced by pleading.

"I must go now," I said, "because my Ma doesn't want me to play here so long and she doesn't know I took Lola out."

I rushed home and carefully opened Ma's wardrobe. Quietly, I pulled her drawers out one by one, and used them as a ladder until I could reach the top. I pushed Lola into the place Ma had made for her.

Holding onto the wardrobe with my hands, I turned around and then jumped onto Ma's bed with a bounce.

"Kathy!" she shouted from the kitchen. "Are you jumping on my bed?"

"No, Ma!" I lied, and quickly pulled her bedspread straight. I closed the wardrobe quickly too, trusting that the door would push all the drawers back in as I heard Ma's shuffling feet coming up the passage.

"What are you doing?" she said in the doorway.

"Nothing, Ma!" I answered.

"Look at my bed!" she snapped and pulled her bedspread off.

Mumbling to herself, she threw it over the bed again.

"Ma?" I asked as she rearranged the frill with her plump hands, "Why can't I have a baby sister?"

"Oh, stop talking nonsense!" she snapped. "Come out of here now. Go play in the back room where I can see you and don't make a noise because my story is coming on!"

CHAPTER 13

Things became hectic in preparation for Christmas.

Apart from Cedric, everyone in our household was on leave. My mother said that she felt disappointed that her work did not have a breaking-up party. She said that it was at this time of the year that she missed her old job because everyone would have dressed up in new clothes and their management would have joined in with the celebrations – eating, drinking and making merry with impromptu entertainment from the girls.

"And there'd be a fashion parade so that everyone could show off their new clothes."

Uncle Reg painted the house room by room. Some days he had friends to help him. Sometimes they got a lot done, sometimes it was "just an excuse to get drunk," as Ma said.

The house was in chaos, with the furniture moved to the centre of the rooms and newspapers spread out on the floor, but the smell of fresh paint made up for the chaos.

Dolores was quite a help too. She helped Ma and Uncle Reg change the curtains and washed the pictures, ornaments and artificial flowers.

My mother and I did all the errands, which mostly took the form of queuing. We stood in a queue at the Post Office to buy stamps for the Christmas cards, we stood in a queue at Wellington's to buy the dried fruit and nuts, again in a queue at the Post Office to buy more stamps for the cards to people who had sent us cards and whom we had forgotten. We stood in queues at Woolworths to buy Christmas underwear and at Ackerman's to buy new net curtaining, in various queues to buy gifts, and finally we stood in the queue on Christmas Eve to buy the leg of pork, the leg of mutton and the other meats for the Christmas meal.

Ma made the Christmas pudding one evening after supper. Chuckling to herself, she poured in some brandy, which she had swiped from Uncle Reg when he was not looking. She had a few tickeys, which she boiled and stirred into the pudding mixture as well.

Before she poured the rich mixture into the unbleached calico cloth in which it was to be boiled, she called us all to come and stir the pudding and make a wish.

"I want to buy a new car," Uncle Reg said. "That's my wish!"

"I wish for a better job in the New Year," my mother said, " – for a firm that has a breaking-up party!"

"I want to fall in love over the festive season," Dolores said, holding her breath and squeezing her eyes tight.

"My wish is a secret," Cedric said, and rolled his eyes heavenward.

"Cedric!" Uncle Reg teased him, laughing.

Ma said, "I wish for prosperity for all my children in the New Year and a wife for Reggie so that my high blood can get better!"

"Gee die ou girl a dop," Cedric said. "Laat sy ook a bietjie jolly voel – is mos festive season, of hoe?"

Everyone laughed and agreed that Ma should have a drink.

Everyone said, "Cheers!" – Ma too.

She took a sip of her drink and pulled a face.

"Ma," I said, softly nudging her; "Ma," trying to get her attention.

"More Coca Cola," she said, gasping. "I don't know how you people can drink this stuff like this!"

"Is lekker, Antie Lenie," Cedric said.

"You've had enough, Cedric!" Ma said.

"Ooh!" Cedric said. "No more for her – sy pick weer op my!"

"Ma," I said again, shaking her arm. "Please, Ma, can I make a wish too?"

"Of course you can," Dolores answered.

Ma gave me the wooden spoon and everyone smiled at me in anticipation.

"Make your wish," Uncle Reg said.

I closed my eyes and solemnly wished for a baby sister to play with and for a bride doll for for Christmas.

"What's your wish?" Dolores prompted me.

"It's a secret," I said, smiling.

"Sê vir hulle, Suster," Cedric said, gulping down another drink.

"This pudding must boil for eight hours," Ma said proudly to Dolores.

"Mmm," Dolores said. "I wish I could have lunch here!"

"Of course you can," Uncle Reg said. "I'm inviting you!"

Ma and my mother stole silent glances at each other and Dolores and Uncle Reg smiled at each other.

CHAPTER 14

Ma was very happy on Christmas Eve. She had her hair in curlers and baked and cooked from early in the morning. She hummed to herself all day, and took a break from her work only for a cup of tea.

In the afternoon my mother and I rushed into Town to buy some decent flowers for the vases. Dolores and Uncle Reg came too, to do some Christmas shopping.

The two of them had become inseparable and often held hands when they thought Ma wasn't looking. That really irritated Ma and my mother, who would gossip about them all the time.

"Can't Reggie pick his company?" my mother would say.

I had bathed and was sitting on the stoep in my pyjamas excitedly waiting for the evening shadow to turn into night so that we could fall asleep and wake to find that it was Christmas morning and that Father Christmas had been.

My mother had taken me to meet him at CTC Building a few days before and he had given me a lucky dip. I was so scared of him and his white beard and was not a bit surprised when I saw my mother paying for the dip and for the photo which I had taken with him. I somehow expected him to be a bit mean. I didn't want to sit on his lap so I stood next to him for the photo. It was not a good photo because I was crying and everyone teased me about it.

I was sorry that I had been so unfriendly towards him because he knew what I wanted for Christmas and now maybe he would not give it to me.

When I am older, I thought afterwards, I won't cry such a lot for silly things. I'll only cry if I fall and hurt my leg and only if it is bleeding a lot.

As the sky darkened, I looked at all the pretty little stars twinkling way above the earth. I tried to locate the biggest one, which I was sure was the one which had led the wise men to the stable where the little baby Jesus lay sleeping in a manger.

I knew it would be the same star because stars don't die.

When I found the biggest star, I closed my eyes and imagined that I was a little shepherd boy in those times, many, many years ago. I sought the same wonder and joy that they had experienced out in the fields where they were watching their flocks. I pretended that I could hear the angels singing and for a moment I think I really did.

After a while, I went to lie on my mother's bed under the window – just for a while – but I fell asleep.

I'm not sure whether it was the early morning church bells pealing in the distance or the hot summer sun shining on my face that woke me, but I was cross with myself for having fallen asleep and having slept right through the night.

I was still lying on my mother's bed. She was fast asleep and became irritable when I tried to wake her, so I left her alone.

Ma wasn't in the room. Her bed was already made up and sported her new, shiny pink bedspread.

In the chair next to the dressing table was a huge parcel wrapped in the prettiest paper, with lots of Father Christmases sitting in sleds with bags of presents being towed behind them and reindeers – lots of them – pulling the sleds.

I gasped in happy anticipation and wondered who the present was for. Perhaps it was for Ma or perhaps my mother – or perhaps, by some strange token of fate, it was for me, left there by Father Christmas himself. I still feared that he might have missed me out because I was rude to him.

I rushed through to the kitchen, but stopped in my tracks in the sitting room. We had a real Christmas tree, all beautifully decorated, and streamers of multi-coloured crinkle paper trimmed across the ceiling, with balloons everywhere.

I walked backwards into the kitchen for fear that it was all just an illusion which would vanish the moment I took my eyes off it.

"Ma," I said, panting now, since words failed me. "Ma … "

"Merry Christmas," Ma said, and gave me a sloppy wet kiss. "Did you see what Father Christmas brought you? It's on the chair."

Who gave us the Christmas tree and who trimmed our sitting room like that?"

"Uncle Reg and his, and his … and Dolores," Ma said, and added in the same breath, "Go and open your present, but remember, Father Christmas told me you must look after it so that you can show it to your children one day."

"I will, Ma," I said, and rushed back to the room again.

CHAPTER 15

I opened my present so carefully because I didn't want to damage even the wrapping paper.

It was the most beautiful bride doll I had ever seen, with eyes that opened and shut and long eyelashes. Her eyes were blue and her hair was yellow-blonde. I could take her clothes and shoes off and put them on again, even her veil.

Ma soon had everyone up for church. Uncle Reg pretended to be sleeping, so she left him alone. We were all dressed and ready to go when Dolores arrived from District Six.

"Where's Reggie, then?" she asked.

"Sleeping," Ma answered.

"Oh no, he's not," Dolores said, and strode through to the back room.

"I'm walking on so long," Cedric said, yawning and wiping the sleep from his eyes – the smell of stale alcohol hanging on his breath.

The church was packed to capacity. Everyone was dressed up in their new Christmas clothes.

The congregation had risen to sing the final Christmas carol, "Hark the Herald Angels Sing," when Uncle Reg and Dolores stole into the back of the church. He had shaven but in his haste he had forgotten to comb his hair. A trickle of blood ran down his face where he had nicked himself while shaving.

"I can't believe that Uncle Reg came to church," I told Ma on our walk home.

"Yes," she said, "even if it is only to hear the last 'Amen' ".

People came in all morning to wish us while Ma and my mother finished the food and Dolores and Cedric swept and dusted. We all wore aprons over our new clothes.

I played on the stoep with Sandra, my new doll, in the

hope that Radia would come out and see her, but they were not at home. I found out afterwards that they had gone to the beach for the day.

Dolores liked Sandra and said that she would teach me to make lots of doll's clothes for her.

Before lunch, Dolores asked me to go home with her to fetch something she had forgotten.

The old couple she lived with in District Six were pleasant. Their home was small and comfortable. It was decorated in the same way that ours was and I gathered that Dolores had done it too.

"This is Reggie's niece," she shouted loudly into the old man's ear.

He cupped his ear and frowned.

"Reggie's niece," she repeated loudly.

"Oh, Berenice," he said, smiling, "Merry Christmas, my girl."

The old lady gave me a glass of home-made ginger beer and put a plate of home-made biscuits on the table.

"Help yourself," she said.

When we left, Dolores kissed both of them.

Lunch was at exactly twelve o'clock, with too much to eat and everyone eating too much, and still there was such a lot of food left over.

My mother and Dolores washed the dishes, while Ma laid the sitting room table with nuts, dried fruits, mixed chocolates, cakes and biscuits for whoever would come to wish us during the afternoon.

I knew my cousins would be coming and decided that since I did not want to be teased by them, Sandra and I would hide away in the bottom of Ma's wardrobe on top of the table cloths and things, and we'd only come out once they had left.

I must have fallen asleep there because the next thing I knew, my mother was lifting me up and putting me to bed.

"Where's everyone?" I asked.

"Gone home," she said softly. "Go to sleep now. We're going to the beach tomorrow."

CHAPTER 16

We were up early – before the sun was properly in the sky. It was an exciting feeling to be awake while the whole world was sleeping.

My mother's friend came to fetch us in his taxi and dropped us at Cape Town station.

We had so much to carry – two old blankets, a huge watermelon and all the food and luxuries left over from Christmas Day, and still Ma's transistor radio and Uncle Reg's guitar.

There were a few people on the station with their own blankets and things, and as the train moved along, more and more people boarded it with their beach things. When we reached Kalk Bay, most of the people got off the train and descended through the subway onto the beach. There were a few people there already, but we were lucky to get a spot under the second tunnel.

Uncle Reg went to bury the watermelon and the cooldrinks in the sand on the beach where the waves broke, so that it would remain cool until we needed them. My mother moaned about all the broken glass in the tunnel.

"A person can cut your feet here," she said.

"I'm going to relax," Ma said, dropping her heavy body onto the spread-out blanket and propping a pillow behind her head.

She kicked her sloffies off, switched the radio on and started fumbling in the biscuit tin.

By mid-morning, every conceivable place to lay a blanket was occupied – right up to the railway line. Brightly coloured blankets were hitched to poles or whatever else presented itself to form makeshift tents in order to provide some shelter from the fierce summer sun.

There were so many people in the water that there was barely enough space to jump up and down and feel the buoyancy of the strangely lukewarm water. There was definitely not enough space to swim in.

Beyond the waves a number of fishing boats were moored. Some big men swam as far as the boats and back again. A few duikers swam around the boats too.

The beach itself was not big at all. It stretched from the harbour on the right to a stormwater drain on the left.

I found myself in a group of children building a sand castle. Every bit of progress we made was shattered by some boys chasing one another – one badly placed foot and our castle collapsed in a heap of sand.

"Let's look for a better place to build our castle," the biggest girl in the group suggested.

Four of us walked over the rocks in search of a bit of beach large enough to build a sandcastle, yet sheltered from rough boys.

We walked as far as the stormwater drain and helped one another onto and over the huge concrete structure. There beyond it was a lovely stretch of uncrowded beach that seemed to go on forever.

We rushed into the waves, splashing one another and laughing.

"Let's build a big castle," the big girl suggested and, picking up a large flat white shell, the kind that people keep in their bird-cages for their birds to sharpen their beaks on, drew a huge circle in the perfectly white sand.

"That is where the moat will be," the girl said.

We sat in the circle and pushed the sand to the centre. We patted it and drew more sand into the centre of the circle until it started taking shape.

Soon we were joined by another group of children. Everyone was helping with the castle. A little girl of about my age gave her bucket to a little boy and instructed him to fetch some shells, which he did. She and I packed the shells around the bottom of the castle while the little boy, on the big girl's instruction, fetched buckets of water to fill the moat. The little girl said that she was also going to school in the New Year, like me.

We took empty ice-cream bakkies and filled them with wet sand, which we patted and slowly emptied on the top of the castle to form "look-outs".

No matter how many times the little boy filled the moat with water, by the time he was back with the next bucket, the water had disappeared.

The little girl and I patted the bottom of the moat as if we could make it watertight. We were laughing and talking happily about our castle when the little girl stiffened and sat upright.

I followed her gaze and saw a man in the distance, running towards us. He was wearing navy blue shorts and seemed to be all shoulders.

"Get away from those coloured children!" he bellowed, and he began kicking our castle down, burying our precious shells underneath the wet sand.

I looked up into his face for some explanation, but there was no answer in his steel-blue eyes.

"... And you children get away from here," he roared, glaring directly at me. "You coloureds have your own beach. Go on! Shoo!" he said, and gave me a shove with his foot.

The big girl had turned on her heel. I watched her scrambling back over the stormwater drain. The man was now dragging the little girl and boy away from me. The little girl was crying and trying to free her arm.

She came running after me.

"The bucket!" she gasped. "My father says we can't play with you because you're coloured."

She took the bucket from me and ran back to where the man was waiting for her.

I looked at the ruins of our castle and wondered what it was that made that man destroy something so beautiful.

CHAPTER 17

Confused, I ran after the big girl and the other children, who were struggling to get over the stormwater drain.

The big girl was out of breath, but laughing all the same. The other children were as bewildered as I was.

"Why are you laughing?" I asked her.

She shook her head and said, "That's not a coloured beach!"

"What's coloured?" I asked.

She ran her forefinger along the outer length of my arm, from my shoulder to my finger tips.

"This," she said, "is coloured. This brown skin is coloured. Those people are white, that is why they have a better beach than we do. We, on this side, we are all coloureds."

A wave of repulsion swept over me. I felt dirty.

I looked at the sea and wished that I could rush into it and wash this brownness from my arms, off my entire body, out of every corner of me.

I ran my fingers along my arm, where the big girl had run her fingers.

"I'll race you to the tunnels," the big girl said, and clambered over the rocks.

I sat down on a flat rock.

"Are you coming?" the big girl called back to me.

I shook my head and she took off again.

I sat on the rock for a while. A group of men were sitting nearby, talking and laughing loudly. The tide was rising, sending huge waves crashing over the harbour wall and driving a spray of white foam into the hot air. Seagulls circled and squawked across the beach, greedily scurrying for hand-outs of yesterday's Christmas lunch. The fishing boats swayed and bobbed on the swelling sea and hundreds of people – coloured people – milled about on the beach like ants in the hot December afternoon sun.

It did not help that there were so many of us. I still wanted to plunge myself into the surf and sink to the depths of the ocean and emerge again – cleaned of this coloured-thing – white as snow.

As the sea gathered momentum with the rising tide, the waves washed ashore, claiming more and more of the beach each time.

I was trapped – there was no escaping it.

All the while that I sat there, I ran my finger in a daze up and down my arm, as if I could erase that terrible feeling of being coloured. But with each stroke of my finger, the big girl's voice echoed in the waves:

"This … is … coloured. This brown skin … "

CHAPTER 18

I remember little else of that day besides Ma moaning that she had to throw all that food away because it was not eaten.

"It's a sin," she kept saying.

The train went clickety-clack, clickety-clack.

Dolores said, "The real sin is that so many animals had to die for nothing – that is the real sin!"

Clickety-clack, clickety-clack.

Uncle Reg and my mother sat back with their heads against the seat and their eyes closed as if asleep.

A lay preacher, tatty Bible in his hand, walked up and down the aisle, warning, "The end is near," and begging everyone – "My brothers and sisters" – to repent "while you still have the time."

Clickety-clack, clickety-clack.

Clickety-clack, clickety-clack.

I stared out of the window at everything, but at nothing, still fingering my arm.

Clickety-clack, clickety-clack.

I remembered what Uncle Reg had said not so long ago. I thought I understood what he had meant, now.

"We don't belong here. This is not our country."

Clickety-clack, clickety-clack.

And my desperate plea:

"Where do we belong, Uncle Reg?"

Where do we belong?

Clickety-clack, clickety-clack.

Clickety-clack, clickety-clack.

PART II

CHAPTER 19

I had given up hope of seeing anything come from Radia's talk of a baby sister and was most surprised to hear from Ma that her mother had had a baby during the night.

"A boy," Ma said.

"A boy?" I asked, surprised. "She said she was getting a sister, Ma!"

Ma laughed. "Children!" she said.

"Can I go over to play with the baby?" I asked Ma.

"Certainly not!" she said. "That is not a toy, it is a real human being, and right now he is not in the mood nor big enough to play with anyone."

"Can I go and see, Ma, please?" I asked.

"No!" Ma said. " You can go later on with me, but you must first help me get done."

I helped Ma do the chores and rushed her on all the time. When we got there Radia was sitting on a chair next to her mother's bed, stroking the head of the little baby lying sleeping next to her mother. Oemie was there, as well as some other ladies. "If there is anything I can do for you," Ma offered to Mrs Abrahams, "just send Radia over to call me. We are all neighbours and must help one another."

"That's true," Oemie said, "but she's got a lot of helpers." I motioned to Radia to come outside and Ma said she must go because she had something on the stove.

"I thought you were going to get a sister," I said to Radia.

"My mother said my sister wasn't ready yet, so she took a baby boy instead," she replied.

"What's the baby's name?" I asked.

"We don't know yet," she answered. "My Daddy must go and fetch a name from the Imam."

"Why must he give the baby a name?" I asked.

"Because we're Moslem," she answered.
I thought about that a little before asking:
"Are Moslem people also coloured?"
"No," Radia said. "We're just Moslem."
"I'm coloured," I said in a hushed voice.
"Oh," Radia answered, as if it didn't matter.

That evening we had a family crisis of our own.

CHAPTER 20

Uncle Peter and Aunty Marjorie came to see Ma about a decision they had taken to apply to be classified white – to be reclassified, as the cliché went.

The process involved a certain amount of humiliation. They had to have a certain number of white people vouch for their characters and had to present themselves to be viewed – so that their skin colour and features could be assessed.

"We are doing it for our children's sakes," Uncle Peter said, trying to convince Ma.

"We want them to have a better future," Aunty Marjorie said, in support of Uncle Peter.

Ma sat down with a sigh. She stared at the floor and ignored everything they had to say about the "very careful decision."

Eventually she spoke, still looking down.

"Bertha, please tell these people to leave, they are not welcome in my home."

"She'll get used to it," Uncle Peter told my mother as they left.

For a few days Ma spoke to no-one. She wore a black dress and didn't even listen to her serials on the radio. One day I came home from school early and found her crying.

I was shattered. I didn't think that I would ever see my Ma crying.

"Ma," I asked, on the verge of tears myself, "why are you crying?"

"I am not your Ma," she said. "I am an empty shell. I live because there is a heart beating in this chest, but that is all. I am like an empty cardboard box – nothing inside – just emptiness. They have killed my spirit!"

I put my head on her lap and watched my frightened tears

fall onto her dress. I thought about what she had said, but didn't quite understand.

"I love you, Ma," I said, "and my mother loves you. And Cedric loves you."

"Yes, my girl," she said, and wiped her face on her apron.

When Uncle Reg came home from sea, Ma told him that he was not to speak about Uncle Peter in the house.

"Your brother's dead," she said coldly.

I was quite alarmed, but my mother told me afterwards that he wasn't really dead, that Ma had decided that he was dead to her.

"What about us?" I asked her. "Is he dead to us, too?"

"I don't know," she answered softly. "I really don't know."

CHAPTER 21

One day at school, the teachers were called to a staff meeting which lasted a long time. Eventually, when the bell rang, the whole school was dismissed. Radia and I walked home together past the shop, where a crowd had gathered. Baai told us that Hendrik Verwoerd, the Prime Minister, had been stabbed, by a white man nogal, and in Parliament too, if you don't mind.

"That's a slap in the face for the Nats," an old man said.

"Things may get better now," someone else offered optimistically.

"No," a pessimist said, "things will get much worse."

When I got home, I told Ma what I had heard. She seemed to be impressed that I even knew who Hendrik Verwoerd was.

"They don't even know that their Prime Minister was stabbed," Ma said of the two white men installing a phone in our house. They were young and friendly, but Ma was not. When they asked her for a cup of coffee, she said she had no coffee in the house and when they said they would have tea instead, she stared at them, making them feel very uncomfortable.

Quietly, they finished their job as fast as they could.

Our phone was a party line which meant that we shared the line with another family further down the road. When we were busy on the line and they picked up their receiver, they could hear our conversation and even join in, although that was unlikely. Likewise when they were using the phone and we picked up our receiver. We had to press a little silver button for dialling tone. We could phone Uncle Reg on the ship and he us, but Ma said that it was too expensive to do unnecessarily.

All of that evening, the radio programmes were interrupted with "pipping" noises so that the latest update on Verwoerd's condition could be given. In the end he died.

One day, Dolores arrived to visit us, in tears. The old people she lived with in District Six were being forcibly removed. They were moving to Wynberg to live with their only daughter.

"... And where do you think she's going to sleep?" Ma asked Uncle Reg, when he went into the kitchen to ask if she could come and stay.

"She can have my bed, Ma," Uncle Reg argued.

"Over my dead body!" Ma snapped. "The two of you have a cheek – not married, but you want her to live under my roof with you like that? I'm sorry, very sorry!"

"Then we'll get married!" Uncle Reg snapped back, banging his fist on the table.

Dolores walked in at that moment and Ma mumbled something about her high blood that was going to kill her one day.

The wedding was nothing special – not like a real wedding at all. Dolores had her hair set at Cedric's hairdresser and borrowed a dress from one of Cedric's friends. They went to the registry office at the court and took Cedric along as a witness.

"... And to think poor Cedric must sleep on the settee because of her," my mother said to Ma.

"Before you could say 'I do', it was over," Dolores said to my mother afterwards. "No silly richer or poorer stuff!"

"What did he say?" my mother asked, trying to seem interested.

"He said, 'Are you Reginald Victor Paulse? Are you Dolores Joan Valentine?' We nodded, he said, 'Sign here,' and 'Witness, sign here,' to Cedric, then he signed it and another official also signed it. That was it – over in less than a minute. Then we got the marriage certificate."

"No blessing!" Ma hissed. "But I wipe my hands!"

There was no reception, but the old couple where Dolores lived, who had not yet moved to Wynberg, made them a special supper. Afterwards, when the word circulated, some of Uncle Reg's friends came around and they all got drunk.

"Do you know what you let yourself in for?" they teased him.

There was no bridal furniture – everything remained the same except that Cedric bought himself a wall bed with a curtain around it. This bed stood against the wall in the sitting room like another mantelpiece with ornaments on it. At night, Cedric opened the curtains, pulled the bed out and made it up for himself to sleep on.

Dolores stopped working immediately because Uncle Reg said, "No wife of mine is going to work – ever! She must stay at home and knit me jerseys!"

Dolores was ecstatically happy. She beamed every time Uncle Reg referred to her as his wife and spoke about the house they were going to buy and all the children they were going to have running around.

"But first, the car," he said.

CHAPTER 22

Although Ma resented Dolores's presence in the house, she was a great help. She took over most of the chores and seemed to create a happy atmosphere in the house as well. She was quite popular with the neighbours, too, running errands for them whenever she was going into Town.

She and I became very close. She plaited my hair for school and I sometimes slept in her bed when Uncle Reg went back to sea.

When the old couple, Uncle Herbie and Auntie Sal, moved to Wynberg, they gave her quite a lot of furniture, so the house became rather cramped, but nevertheless she made the back room very pleasant and comfortable. She liked fresh flowers on her dressing-table and we often walked into Town to buy some. At night she would put the flowers on the kitchen table – "Because they will use up all the oxygen and we will suffocate," she would say.

We spoke about many things. She told me that I was a lot like her. Her mother had also had her before she married.

"I used to see him every few years, but I didn't know when I would see him again," she said of her father. "He always brought me something," she smiled, "but it was always miles too small for me."

We lay there for a while and watched the moonlight light up the mountain. It was a magnificent sight. Of course it irritated Ma that Dolores slept with her curtains open, but Dolores was not concerned in the least.

"I don't think I have a father," I said, breaking into Dolores's nostalgic stillness.

"You must have a father," she said, and set about explaining the facts of life to me.

She made it sound so romantic that I could actually see

Adam and Eve falling in love in the Garden of Eden. She stressed that it only happened when two people fell in love.

"So you can see that we are all made out of love," she mused.

I wondered who the man was who had fallen in love with my mother and wondered if he knew about me.

"… And then when I was eleven years old, my mother married someone else who didn't know about me. That was just after she put me with Auntie Sal and Uncle Herbie. They were actually friends of friends of my grandmother's."

She smiled again, the moonlight dancing on her deep dimples.

"She also visited very occasionally and also the things that she brought were miles too small for me, but I kept them for years because it was like having some part of her with me. She promised that she would fetch me one day, but it didn't happen. I used to long for her so – especially when Marilyn, the old people's grown-up daughter, used to threaten to leave home because of me. I'm sure if my mother could, she would have fetched me, I don't know what kept her away. Eventually that is what happened. She just stayed away. I haven't heard from her for years. I wouldn't know where to begin looking for her. Someone told Auntie Sal once that she is living in Johannesburg. I used to think she used to stay away because I used to cry so much when she wanted to leave. I don't know. I only hope she's happy."

She sighed again, her eyes brimming with tears.

"You know, the old people were very good to me and loved me as much as I loved them, but it's not the same. Deep down you know you don't belong to them and there was a lot of jealousy with Marilyn – even after she left home. She would come in there and demand to know who paid for the food I ate and who had bought me the clothes I was wearing. Sometimes she would bring Uncle Herbie a chocolate and make him swear on the Bible that he would not give me a piece of it. Shame, after she left, he would quietly slip out and go to the shop to buy me a chocolate and he wouldn't eat his chocolate – he'd leave it in the drawer for Auntie Sal and after a few days, she would give it to me anyway."

I found my mind wandering, for the first time, to a man, nameless and faceless – living somewhere – who was my father. I tried to find some emotion to feel towards this man, but there was nothing. I felt nothing.

Dolores chattered on about the unpleasantness of Marilyn, who was at least twelve years her senior. Marilyn stopped speaking to her mother after Dolores came to live with them, and had only started speaking to her again in the last two years, since she had become converted.

"You know," Dolores was saying, "sometimes my mother would send a message that she was coming to fetch me and I would wait for her, all dressed up. I'd sit at the window for hours until late at night – just waiting for her, but she did not come. I wonder why she did that? Why she said she would come and then did not?"

She lay there, fresh tears coursing down her face in the moonlight. I took the towel off the back of the chair and gave it to her. Gratefully, she took it and wiped her face.

My heart went out to this little girl sitting at the window waiting for a mother who didn't show up, this little girl at the centre of a family feud, and I realised how lucky I was to have all the people I had around me.

Maybe that was why I never thought about my father – even to admit that he had to exist.

I was curious, though, and plucked up the courage to ask Ma about him.

"You've been talking to Dolores again!" Ma snapped at me, and refused to discuss it.

"Let sleeping dogs lie," she said.

CHAPTER 23

I enjoyed having Dolores around. She bought things like Elastoplast and real toilet paper and ointment that smelled like bubblegum, which was a far cry from the Gentian Violet and Friar's Balsam that Ma used to put on my knees when I grazed them.

I liked the smell of Friar's Balsam, but it burnt like nothing on earth and Ma would dab it roughly and scold me at the same time.

"It's because you don't walk," she'd say. "You have to run all the time. What's the rush, anyway?" Or, "It's because you don't pick up your feet properly. You are always falling over your feet!"

Dolores took me out a lot during school holidays. We would get up early and I'd help her with the household chores by doing things like shaking the mats out and drying the dishes. She'd put the meat on and peel the potatoes so that when Ma got up, she'd have to do only her own room and add something in the pot for supper – peas and carrots, shredded cabbage, tomato paste or curry powder.

One day Dolores decided that we would visit Aunty Sal and Uncle Herbie in Wynberg.

"I must go and see how they are. I worry about them a lot. If we go early, we can go to bioscope in Wynberg in the afternoon. They have a nice new bioscope there – actually, it's a theatre."

"Good!" I said.

"I think it's a Beatles film – *A Hard Day's Night*," she said.

Dolores loved the Beatles. She knew all their names and all their songs. She said she was going to buy their new LP for Uncle Reg when he returned from sea. Her favourite song was "Exclusively Yours".

My mother and Cedric liked the Beatles too, but Ma said they were evil and just made a lot of noise.

We took the bus as far as the Cogill's Hotel in Wynberg and then walked through a subway and down York Road as far as Sussex Road, through to Ottery Road and then a little distance to the left. The old lady's directions were precise.

The house had a long veranda, but it was so dark because it was almost grown closed with unkempt creepers. It looked like the palace in the Sleeping Beauty story when the prince found it.

Innocent purple morning glories crept along the wire fence on the side of the house too, bowing their heads in obedience to the wind.

Dolores knocked on the door and we waited. She knocked again, this time a little louder, and frowned at me when it remained unanswered.

"Open the door," I said eagerly.

Dolores pushed it open slowly. There was a long passage with a door at the end of it. We stepped inside and walked down the dark passage slowly on tip-toes. The eyes of the people in the yellowing photographs that lined the wall of the passage, possibly relatives from an earlier era, followed us as we walked.

"Coo-ee," Dolores called, opening the back door since there was no sign of life in the house.

We stepped down into the backyard and jumped back in horror as the hugest, meanest-looking Alsatian charged at us.

I grabbed at Dolores's dress and froze as the dog snarled and growled, baring his teeth, ready to pounce at the slightest provocation.

"Bruno!" a strange-sounding voice called, and he started wagging his tail, his eager eyes still on us, his teeth still bared, saliva dripping onto the ground. My clammy hands still clung to Dolores's dress, my heart was pounding, my mouth dry.

"Sit, Boy!" the voice commanded, and Bruno, wagging and mumbling, sank back into a sitting position, his eyes still intently on us.

"He won't bite," the woman said as she came down the garden path with an armful of washing.

"He's just playful, that's all. He's still a puppy, aren't you, Bruno? Go play now!"

Bruno turned and scampered off down the garden path and lost himself in the tall foliage.

"The madam's not here," the woman said. "Only the old missus."

"Where is the old missus?" Dolores asked.

"The madam, she's gone to the shop to buy something. She'll be just now here."

"Where is the old missus?" Dolores repeated, an edge to her voice now.

The woman said something about the wind being just right for washing and led us into the house.

"Come, I take you to the old missus," she said.

CHAPTER 24

The room was small, dark and musty. The old lady sat in a rickety chair with her hands in her lap, staring into space. Her eyes had a far-away look. She turned to face us, but didn't recognise us.

Dolores threw her arms around her.

"Aunty Sal," she said, "it's me – Dolores!"

The old lady looked at Dolores closely and frowned.

"Is it you, Dolores?" she asked.

"Yes, Aunty Sal, it's me. How are you? Are you well? Where's Uncle Herbie?"

The maid stood in the doorway and looked up the passage towards the front door. She dropped her put-on English accent when she spoke.

"Shame," she said, "sy's nie gelukkig hierso nie. Haar dogter is nie so lekker saam met haar nie."

The old lady was crying as she clung to Dolores. The tears were running down Dolores' face too. I felt like crying also, but I had no share in the emotions in the room so I went to look out of the window instead.

The ground seemed to go on forever and had countless fruit trees. There was a loquat tree laden with ripe fruit. A flock of greedy black starlings sat in the tree picking at the ripe fruit.

The maid was standing behind me.

"Stroopsoet!" she said, "But the madam don't want no-one to pick. But wait, I pick you some quickly before she come."

She rushed out into the garden, with the dog jumping clumsily around her. "Okay, Bruno," she said, "Okay, Boy," as she hurriedly picked the loquats, sending the birds scattering into the air. They perched in a tall, thick mulberry tree at the other side of the garden, twittering anxiously. "Steek weg!"

the maid said as she hurried back into the house. "Gou, she's now-now here!"

She stuffed the loquats down the bodice of my dress against my skin! I was too shocked to object as she hastily did up the buttons of my jersey.

"As julle weer kom is die moerbeie ryp," she said. "Shame, sy's lonely. Julle moet weer kom. Haar dogter is nie lekker saam met haar nie."

Dolores and Aunty Sal were sitting on the bed. Aunty Sal held Dolores's hands in her lap. Every now and again she dabbed at her eyes with a large white handkerchief.

Slowly and carefully I made my way to the chair at the window and sat down. The loquats tickled my stomach as I moved. I pictured coming there in a white dress without a jersey to cover it and this woman shoving ripe mulberries down my dress. I'd come out in purple blobs. The dress would have the measles! It seemed so funny, I wanted to laugh. Imagine a dress with measles. I let out a snigger, but suppressed the really naughty loud laugh that was sitting in my throat.

The maid was talking to Dolores.

"Shame, sy's oud en jy weet hulle wil net tee drink. Shame, she just wants tea all day long, but her daughter says, 'No, you can have tea when I have tea!'"

"Shoo ! Go !" Aunty Sal said to the maid, "Go away ! She has no right to talk like that, after all she works for Marilyn. Ungrateful creature – where's her loyalty?"

Just then the front door burst open and Marilyn, Aunty Sal's daughter, came in huffing and puffing from the walk and laden with heavy parcels which she dropped on the floor in the passage. She shouted for the maid as she strode down the passage. She stopped at Aunty Sal's door and looked in, but didn't greet us, nor did she give us a chance to greet her. "She's having a hard time!" Aunty Sal said, "She doesn't mean to be rude!"

She put her hand under her pillow and pulled out half a packet of Marie biscuits.

"Here, girl," she said, handing me one.

"Where's Uncle Herbert?" Dolores asked.

Aunty Sal started crying again.

"He goes to the house every day," she said, catching her breath.

"At least, that's what he says. There's no house there any more – they've bulldozed the houses flat – it was in *The Argus* and *The Herald*."

"Then where does he go?" Dolores asked.

"I don't know," Aunty Sal said softly, "I wish I knew."

CHAPTER 25

It was difficult getting Aunty Sal to understand that we had to go home. Dolores promised her that we would come again.

"... And when Reggie comes home, he's going to buy a car – a Valiant, then he'll bring me every week," Dolores said, trying to offer her some comfort.

Aunty Sal clung to Dolores and sobbed.

"Take me with you," she cried, "I miss you, I miss my house and my neighbours. I miss the harbour and the smell of the sea. I wish I was dead!" she said, letting go of Dolores.

"One day, when Reggie and I buy a house, you'll come and live with us, Aunty Sal. You'll see, it won't be long."

The working people were coming home from work already when we walked up to the bus-stop. Dolores walked so fast that I had to trot to keep up with her.

We sat upstairs in the bus right at the back, in the corner. There were very few people on the bus.

Dolores sat staring out of the window while I manoeuvred the loquats out of my clothes one by one, enjoying the juicy sweetness of the fruit and collecting a pile of the shiny, copper-coloured, marble-like pips in my lap.

"We didn't go to bioscope," I said, touching Dolores on her arm.

"We'll go another time!" she said, turning towards me. "When it comes to the Gem, perhaps. Hell's teeth! Did you eat all of that? Where are the skins?"

"I ate them," I said, somewhat alarmed.

She smiled.

"Your stomach is going to run," she said, laughing. "All night, right through the night."

I felt that, cramps and all, it was a small price to pay for the pleasure I had had from the loquats, so I was not too much concerned.

Dolores was staring out of the window again. A red glow spread across the sky, reflecting on the wispy clouds.

"Are you worried about Aunty Sal?" I asked.

"Yes," she said. "I wish Reggie and I had a house so that I could look after her and Uncle Herbie. I wonder where he goes to every day?" She took a deep breath.

"Do you believe what the woman said about Aunty Sal's daughter?" I asked.

"Yes, but she shouldn't speak out of the house. It's a very ugly thing to do."

"Why didn't they buy another house?" I asked her.

She laughed. "The council paid them only the municipal value – perhaps just enough to put down as a deposit, if that. No, they must forget about buying another house. Besides, they're pensioners, where would they get a bond?"

Dolores said that she felt very bitter towards the government and towards white people in general. She said that they were going to move all coloured people from decent areas to remote areas, where we'd all be lumped together – just like the Africans are.

"If I were your Ma, I'd sell now while she can still get a better price for the house and buy somewhere like Grassy Park. If she doesn't, she won't be able to buy again."

"Ma will never move," I said. "She told my mother and me that they will have to carry her out in a box before she moves."

"Uncle Herbert also said that," she mused. "Shame, they were too old for such trauma. They lived there all their married life, you know. Uncle Herbert bought the house from a Jewish man he used to work for – and they were so proud of that house, they kept it beautifully. It was really a home."

The white ticket conductor came upstairs and looked around.

He smiled at me and I frowned, avoiding his dazzling blue eyes. He winked at me, still smiling.

67

I looked at Dolores, but she was deliberately looking out of the window again.

"Pretty girls like you shouldn't be travelling alone in the dark," the conductor said, nudging Dolores's foot with his own.

She turned towards him slowly, her green eyes flashing like a cat's in the night.

"Voetsek!" she spat at him.

Sheepishly, the conductor turned on his heel and went downstairs.

"You can't blame all white people," I whispered, feeling sorry for the conductor.

"Oh yes, you can!" Dolores said angrily, "They have the vote, which means that they have the privilege of being heard. They can stop it if they want to. They're all the same – each one feathering his own nest. They are bullies – greedy, sadistic, cowardly bastards!"

CHAPTER 26

It was pitch dark when we walked up the road.

"Ma is going to moan," Dolores said, clutching my hand to pull me along.

Everyone had eaten already and the kitchen was tidied when we got home. Ma and my mother pounced on Dolores, who was so out of breath that she was panting.

"How dare you?" they shouted at her, "How dare you? What gives you the right?"

Dolores didn't have a chance to say anything. She went pale, then red, then burst into tears. She fled to her room and closed the door.

"Verskoon my," Cedric said with distaste, and went to stand on the stoep.

"And you, young lady," my mother said, "Don't think that you are big just because you go to school."

"Go and wash your hands and come and eat," Ma said.

When my mother pulled my jersey off, all of my loquat pips fell out of my sleeve and onto the floor.

"In the bin, every one of them, do you want to bring ants?"

I was already in trouble, so I dared not argue. On my hands and feet I gathered the pips together and dropped them into the bin one by one, listening for each clunk.

We had cabbage bredie for supper – not my favourite food. I told Ma that I wasn't hungry and really was not.

She said two words in that voice of hers:

"Eat it!"

I ate very slowly, swallowing each mouthful against my will. The fat was setting on the plate, but I sat there until I had finished the very last grain of rice.

I lay in bed listening to Cedric telling someone that the weather was changing, and wondered if Dolores had eaten her supper. I thought of my loquat pips lying in the bottom of the bin and about the people of our country being divided into us and them. I began to understand what Uncle Reg had meant when he said we didn't belong here – that this was not our country.

I had one of those stupid dreams where everything kept changing into something else. We were sitting on the bus, Marilyn was the conductor, then we weren't sitting on the bus any more, we were sitting in the bioscope and the conductor was on the screen eating loquats, then the big Alsatian dog was on the screen, then he was chasing us up the road in the dark. We ran so fast, the dog's breath on the back of my neck, so fast that my side hurt. It hurt so badly that it woke me.

Everything was still and quiet and dark – only my mother's breathing and Ma's uneven snoring penetrated the night. My stomach cramped in strong spasms. It hurt badly and I knew I'd have to go to the toilet, but I didn't want to wake Ma or my mother because they would blame Dolores. I lay still for a while, trying to wish them away, but the cramps kept coming.

Carefully, quietly and very scared, I got out of bed, very much aware that some strange evil could grab my feet from under the bed. Tip-toeing and listening for strange sounds, I made my way down the passage. I could feel the eyes of my deceased ancestors, whose pictures hung on the wall down the passage, following my every move. I peered into the lounge, expecting someone to jump out from behind the door or under the couch to say, "Got you!"

Cedric ground his teeth in his sleep.

"Cedric," I whispered, but he didn't hear me. "Cedric!"

There was no way that I was going outside on my own.

"Cedric!" I said into his ear as I threw myself on top of him.

"What's the matter?" he said, still grinding his teeth and turning his back on me.

"Cedric," I said again, "wake up."

He sat up and looked at me.

"Take me to the lavvy, please," I begged.

He mumbled and shuffled his feet into his slippers.

"Come," he said, picking me up.

Dolores's light was on when we passed through the kitchen.

CHAPTER 27

There was a slight breeze outside. The moon was full and lit up the sky. Here and there a star peeked out and was gone again as dark clouds and lighter clouds raced across the sky.

I sat on the toilet with Cedric hurrying me on in the doorway and Spotty jumping up at Cedric's bare legs.

Relief was short-lived. I thought all my insides were passing out of me with every constricting cramp.

Loquats!

When we went into the house Dolores's light was still on. Impulsively I opened the door, Cedric peering into the room too.

"What are you doing?" I asked her.

"Writing a letter to Reggie," she answered, looking very glum.

"Moet jou nie upset met die ou girl nie," Cedric said, and plonked himself in a squatting position on the bed. "Sy is maar so."

An awkward silence followed in which Dolores put her letter down on the pedestal next to the bed.

"Tell Cedric about Bruno," I said.

Dolores laughed, throwing her head back. I jumped into bed with her and egged her on as she told him about the day's events.

She told him about how sad Aunty Sal was and what a pity it was that they had to leave their house.

"She's gone so thin and old," she said. "And then there's Uncle Herbert, who disappears every morning and comes home after dark. Aunty Sal says he doesn't wash himself any more and wears the same clothes for days on end. What's happening to them?"

Cedric told her about some of his clients telling him of an

old man who sat on the pavement every day from morning to night where his home used to be.

"The bulldozers and things go deurmekaar, but he sits there where he sits – on the pavement outside where his house used to be."

"What's happening to this country of ours?" Dolores said sadly.

"The government is trying to create a Colouredstan, like the Bantustans," Cedric said. "They are worse than the Nazis – no respect for human life!"

"Where will it all end?" Dolores said softly.

"It will end, make no mistake," Cedric said, "after a lot of pressure from the rest of the world and a lot of bloodshed here. It has to change – dis onmenslik. White people too must examine their consciences and put pressure on the government to put things right. How they sleep in their comfortable houses in white areas, I don't know!"

"They won't put pressure on the government," Dolores said, "why should they? They're all sitting pretty with the best of everything: job reservation, the amenities – everything, and to think that they are the minority."

"Yes," said Cedric, "we are the silent majority."

"What about African people?" Dolores said. "They have a raw deal – look at the pass laws!"

"Yes," Cedric said. "Those men don't know what it is to see their children grow up because their families cannot live with them out of the Transkei and they'll never own property in their own country. Often the men have women here in Cape Town as well as a wife at home."

"That's terrible!" Dolores said. "If Reggie was to take another woman, I don't know what I will do!"

"We all pay rates and taxes," Cedric said, "but we have no say in the country. And what do they do with the money they take from us? Spend it on defence, the farmers and on keeping apartheid alive!"

He yawned and pulled his sweater over his bare legs.

"Hey, look at the time!" he said. "I must get some sleep."

"It's weekend tomorrow," Dolores said.

"For you, maybe," Cedric said, "but Sister, I'm early on the job. Saturday is my busy day and I've got two weddings to do." He went out and switched the light off.

"I wonder if that old man is Uncle Herbert," Dolores said. "I'll have to go down there to see."

I was very sad for Dolores. I knew she loved those old people very much.

"How can a whole country stand by and watch this brutality?" she said. "What has happened to the hearts of men and why does God allow it?"

CHAPTER 28

Radia's baby brother, Sedick, was growing fast and naughty. Since Radia was the eldest girl, she was called "Tittie" in their family, and Sedick knew to call her "Tittie" too. Poor Radia didn't have much time to play any more. She went to Moslem school or Madressa every afternoon and when she was home, her mother called her all the time to "see what Dickie is doing."

Her mother had said that, since she was so obliging, when it was Radia's birthday she and Aunty Mariam would take all the children to the Community Chest Carnival in Wynberg and that I could come along too. Radia said that they and Aunty Mariam went every year and Sumaya, Radia's cousin, said that there was a merry-go-round and we could go on the swings that went so fast, you'd have to hold very tight or you would fall off and could die.

Radia and I were very excited and couldn't wait for the two weeks to pass. My mother bought me a new dress for the occasion and gave me a one rand note to spend on myself and a one rand note for Radia as a birthday present.

Finally the magical Saturday dawned. We took a bus to Newlands where Aunty Mariam and Sumaya lived. Of course, Sedick made us late by dirtying himself and having to be changed again.

Sumaya and her mother were waiting for us at the bus-stop, so we did not get off the bus. Instead, they boarded the bus and we continued on our way to Wynberg. All along the way, posters advertising the Carnival were displayed on poles at the bus-stops.

The bus conductor helped us to carry the pushcart off the bus and he was so kind, he even put it together for Mrs Abrahams while holding up the bus and its load of passengers.

The queue at Maynardville was long and Sedick was impatient but Radia, Sumaya and I were so excited because we could see the merry-go-round from outside in the queue and we could hear the strains of the string band and the laughter of other children.

There seemed to be some confusion at the gate where we had to buy the tickets and the patrons behind us started grumbling that we were holding the queue up.

"What's the matter?" Radia asked her mother.

"They won't let us in," she said, while Aunty Mariam argued with the ticket clerk.

"I've been coming here every single year," she shouted at the top of her voice.

"Why don't they want us to go in?" Radia asked her mother, dismayed.

"All the years my money was good enough," Aunty Mariam said. "Now they only want white people's money!"

"I want to go in!" Sumaya cried.

"Sumaya, shut up!" her mother snapped, dragging her away.

Patrons in the queue shook their heads and mumbled while others looked the other way.

"I want to go on the swings!" Sumaya screamed.

Aunty Mariam lost her temper and gave Sumaya a few hard smacks on her bottom.

The uniformed man at the gate continued doing his job and said in disgust to the people he was attending to:

"People think I make the rules."

We walked away, Aunty Mariam still scolding that her money was the same colour as anyone else's and that she wouldn't infect anyone with her brownness and that she was a better person than a lot of white people.

"Miessies, dit baat nie Miessies staan in die queue nie," she told a woman who was standing further down the queue with her children – "is net vir wittes dié jaar."

The woman frowned and looked around her at the other patrons, who awkwardly looked away, and then she took her children's hands and told them that they would not be going to the Carnival this year.

"Why?" her son asked.

"Because I say so!" she snapped.

We walked to the bus-stop at Woolworths and then Mrs Abrahams said we would be going to Claremont Gardens to see the brides since it was still Radia's birthday and we could still enjoy it.

But it was already an unhappy birthday and would always bring back unhappy memories for me and Radia, even though the brides at Claremont Gardens looked very pretty.

CHAPTER 29

My mother said she would not like to have a marriage like Dolores's and Uncle Reg's.

"She sees her husband only a few times a year. I want my man to be home every night."

"Will you get married one day?" I asked her.

"If somebody wants me, I may," she said.

"You won't get married," Ma said.

Dolores's pregnancy came to me as a shock, but she was so ecstatic, so I was happy for her. I wasn't jealous of the little baby growing inside of her, how could I be? Uncle Reg was happy too. He said he knew it was a boy and had great plans for him.

My mother knitted the sweetest, cutest little matinée jackets and bootees "for those sweet little feet" in the palest lemon and snowiest white. She chattered tenderly and happily to Dolores about the time when she had been pregnant with me. It made me feel so special, so wanted. Ma said that Dolores mustn't knit herself because "the cord will get twisted around the baby's neck."

Nurse said it was an old wives' tale, "but you can never be too careful, strange things do happen."

Uncle Peter had taken to phoning my mother regularly from his office on Saturday mornings. Ma pretended not to be interested in who was on the phone, but I'm sure she knew it was Uncle Peter. Sometimes my mother would tell her of the things he said, but she would not show any interest. She listened, but she did not comment and not once did she say that she did not want to hear.

Apparently Uncle Peter was doing very well for himself. He had worked his way up to become the manager of the place where he worked and had bought himself a beautiful house in Pinelands. "Peter wants us to come see his house," my mother said to Ma.

"Peter wants us to see his house," my mother repeated.

Ma gave her a cold, sarcastic stare.

The night that Uncle Peter came to fetch us to see his house was dark and gloomy, with the threat of rain. It was midweek, but luckily during the school holidays, so that I did not have to worry about being up late. We waited on the stoep for him all evening, Dolores, my mother and me. "He's not coming," Dolores kept saying.

"He said he'd come, so he will come," my mother argued, trying not to appear as agitated as she was.

Eventually we gave up, Dolores first.

"I'm going to bed!" she said.

"Ma's asleep already!" I told my mother.

"Yes," she said, "something must have happened."

We were in our pyjamas, about to get into bed, when we heard the hooter.

"It's him!" I said, pulling back the curtain.

I raced down the passage to tell Dolores. Luckily she was still in her dress at the dressing-table, writing another letter to Uncle Reg.

"There's no time for you to change," my mother said to me. "Just put your gown on."

It was the first time that Uncle Peter had met Dolores. He seemed to like her, as he kept looking at her in his mirror. Dolores smiled shyly every time their eyes met.

"He's so much like Reggie," she whispered to me.

"It's rude to whisper in company," Uncle Peter joked.

Dolores blushed and my mother yawned.

"We're just about there," Uncle Peter whispered as he switched the car lights off.

We drove a few yards in darkness and then he eased the car into a driveway. The house was in total darkness. In fact, so were all the houses in the street, as if all the residents were sound asleep.

"Shh," he whispered, "we don't want to wake the

neighbours," as he gently pushed his door closed and cringed as I banged the back door. I didn't mean to bang it, it just happened.

"Kathy!" my mother said.

"Shh," Uncle Peter said, putting his finger to his lip and frowning as he gently opened the unlocked front door.

CHAPTER 30

Aunty Marjorie stood in the dark passage in her lilac dressing gown and fluffy lilac slippers. She nodded her head at my mother and Dolores and led the way to the kitchen at the back of the house. I looked at her all the time, hoping that she'd look my way so that I could greet her, but she didn't. The kitchen light was on, but the rest of the house was in darkness.

Everyone stood around in the kitchen, looking at one another as if expecting something to happen.

"So, show them around," Aunty Marjorie said to Uncle Peter.

Uncle Peter led us through the three-bedroomed house in the darkness. My cousins, Christopher and Edward, were asleep in one bedroom and one was used as a dining-room. On the sideboard stood the sail ship in the bottle that Uncle Reg had brought home from a trip. He had said that he had made it himself, but when I had asked him how he had managed to get the whole ship through the neck of the bottle with all its sails perfectly hoisted, he had said, with a gleam in his eyes: "That's my secret!"

Our quick guided tour of the house was over and we returned to the kitchen. I still looked intently at Aunty Marjorie for an opportunity to catch her eye, so that she could acknowledge me.

Everyone stood around in uncomfortable silence, with the sound of the fridge motor emphasizing the uneasiness.

My mother and Dolores looked at the walls, the ceiling and the floor as if they were examining something at an exhibition. They looked at each other and then looked at the walls again.

"It's getting late," Aunty Marjorie said. "You'd better take them home."

"Yes," Uncle Peter said, "It's almost twelve o'clock and it's work tomorrow."

We drove home from Pinelands in virtual silence. Every now and then Uncle Peter would say something like: "It's going to rain tomorrow – that's for sure!"

I don't know whether it was the smell of the vinyl seats, or the sickly sweet smell of the air-freshener block at the back, or a combination of the two, but something tormented the pit of my stomach and I wanted to be sick. I thought I'd try to keep it in until we got home, but I couldn't.

"Stop the car," Dolores said quickly, "Kathy's going to be sick!" The car chugged to a halt and Dolores flung the back door open. I leaned over her and everything came out – everything and nothing, but a purging all the same.

My mother wiped my face with her handkerchief.

"Do you want to sit on my lap?" she asked.

"No," I said, and snuggled up to Dolores on the back seat.

"We're nearly home," my mother said.

"Dolores likes children, hey?" Uncle Peter asked as he started the car engine.

"Yes," my mother said, "that's why she's having one of her own."

"Is she?" Uncle Peter asked, looking at Dolores in the rear-view mirror. "And you can't even see anything!"

"Of course you can!" Dolores said, easing her hand over her swollen belly.

I rushed into the house with my mother behind me. We left Dolores to say the formal goodbyes to Uncle Peter.

I was gargling at the kitchen sink when Dolores came through to the back. The sound of Uncle Peter's car receded into the distance.

"He's so much like Reggie!" Dolores said, starry-eyed.

"Reggie would never have done that!" my mother said. "He didn't want his neighbours to know that he had coloured people in his house and what is *he* anyway? No, my dear, he is *not* like Reggie!"

"It wasn't him!" Dolores argued. "It was his wife –

miserable hag that she is, she didn't even offer us tea. Did you see how she was looking at me? Meanwhile, Peter tells me that I can easily pass for white and that Reggie and I must apply to be reclassified like them for the baby's sake."

"That is so pathetic," my mother said. "So pathetic."

"And so?" Ma asked as we climbed into bed.

My mother told her how unfriendly Aunty Marjorie had been and about all the lights being off.

"She didn't even offer us a seat, never mind tea!" she said.

"You will take his part because blood is thicker than water," Ma said, "but he is the man. He makes the decisions. What kind of man is he? You mustn't blame Marjorie."

A moment of light flashed through the room, followed by the almighty roar of thunder.

"The washing!" Ma said.

"I'll get it quickly," my mother said, jumping to her feet.

She returned a few minutes later, quite out of breath.

"There's nothing on the line."

"Dolores must have brought it in," Ma said.

My mother climbed into bed next to me. Her feet were like ice and I drew myself away from her.

The heavens opened. Heavy drops of rain pelted down on the tin roof like the thundering feet of an army of angry warriors.

"I hope Peter's home already," my mother said, snuggling up to me with her cold feet.

"Serves him right if he isn't!" Ma said.

CHAPTER 31

Pregnancy suited Dolores. Her hair was soft and shiny and tied back in a ponytail. Her skin glowed and there was a certain radiance about her. The little bump growing beneath her clothes was now clearly visible.

One Friday night the phone rang and Dolores answered. "Uncle Herbie's dead," she said softly as she replaced the receiver.

"What?" Ma asked, alarmed.

"They found him lying dead in the subway," Dolores said, with tears in her eyes. "I'll have to go through to Aunty Sal."

She stood there looking down at the floor, tears rolling freely down her face onto her dress. She did nothing to stop them, nor did she make an attempt to dry them.

She looked so helpless and alone in her grief.

"You can't go now," my mother said. "It's too late. Besides, who will take you?"

"What about Peter?" Dolores asked, looking up.

My mother and Ma looked at each other.

"Peter would never come," my mother said. "Tomorrow's Saturday. We'll take a bus through – me, you and Kathy. We'll all go."

Dolores nodded and retired to her bedroom to write another letter to Uncle Reg.

Wynberg Main Road was busy with Saturday morning shoppers. It seemed so strange to see so many people doing their business when someone had died in their area. When Oemie Davids had died, everyone, but everyone had been at her house. The same when Mrs Petersen's mother died.

Why must people die? And now Uncle Herbie!

Perhaps the people in Wynberg were different. Perhaps they didn't know Uncle Herbie well enough to mourn his death. Or perhaps I just expected too much of the people in Wynberg.

There were a few of Aunty Sal and Uncle Herbie's old neighbours sitting in the sitting room drinking tea.

Aunty Sal sat in a chair next to the piano. She looked so composed for a grieving widow, and said the strangest thing to Dolores.

"Don't cry for him now, my girl. He died a long time ago, when they put him out of his house. That's when he died. He's at peace now where no-one can take anything away from him. No, no-one can hurt him now. He's finally found his peace."

She didn't cry, but her eyes were brimming with watery tears, which she dabbed at ever so sedately with a white handkerchief.

The other people mumbled amongst themselves and nodded their heads.

"He's at peace now," people said intermittently.

"Where's Marilyn?" someone asked.

Aunty Sal answered. "She's in bed. This doctor – Magan, I think it is – came to the house and gave her something to make her sleep."

She paused and repeated: "She took it bad, you know, they found him lying on his face in the subway – they said he must have fallen down the steps and knocked his head. Poor Marilyn, poor girl, she took it bad."

All morning people came in to offer their condolences. Some people sympathised with Dolores too, some mistook her for Marilyn, some sympathised with everyone in the room.

A man of about Uncle Peter's age said something that made everyone sit up in anger.

"They killed him," the man said. "They killed him – they brought him to his knees and they spat in his face, they kicked him down and left him to die! Every white man in this country is guilty of Uncle Herbie's death. His home was his pride and they just took it away like that – for what?"

85

"They'll never treat white people like that!" the man's lady companion said. "They will never put up with it!"

Mumblings of, "They killed him," and, "They'll never treat white people like that," passed over the lips of the mourners. Anger began to gather in every pair of eyes until it hung in the air like a thick fog.

Not one white person was to be excused. They were all guilty of this heinous crime. If they hadn't taken part, they had stood by and watched.

"Those bastards operating the bulldozers not only destroyed their homes, they destroyed their lives too."

I could not resist the anger of this tiny gathering of mourners: it came at me like a whirlwind and became my own. I felt it stirring through me, finding its way into my marrow and fermenting there.

All day, people came and went and the anger smouldered.

Aunty Sal sat upright, tired and confused in the armchair, which seemed too big and ugly for her diminutive form. Dolores sat on the arm of the chair, looking forlorn.

Eventually my mother caught Dolores's eye and tapped on her wristwatch.

Dolores got up to leave and hugged Aunty Sal as if she would never see her again.

"Don't cry," Aunty Sal said, stroking her hair. "Don't cry. You must look after yourself and the baby. Remember to look at something beautiful every day and think beautiful thoughts so that you have a beautiful child."

"I'll see you on Tuesday at the funeral," Dolores said.

"Oh, yes ..." Aunty Sal said, as if she had not yet given any thought to a funeral for poor deceased Uncle Herbie.

CHAPTER 32

We waited a while for the bus.

"I'm lekker hungry now," Dolores said.

"Let's buy some hot fish and chips at the fish shop over there," my mother suggested.

"What if the bus comes?" Dolores asked.

"Just tell him to wait," my mother laughed.

She and I went to the fish shop opposite the terminus and bought a parcel of fish and chips and three pickled onions.

There was a juke-box in the shop and some young men were singing and dancing to the music which they had selected. They all whistled at my mother.

"I can't stand any longer," Dolores said when we returned. She plonked herself down on the pavement.

"You'll get inflammation," my mother warned her, laughing again.

"Come, open the chips," Dolores said, "before I starve to death."

We stood around the newspaper parcel and ate with our hands. The chips were big and soggy and had a lot of vinegar and salt sprinkled on them, the fish was enveloped in a thick crispy batter and the pickled onion was crunchy and sour.

"Nothing for us?" a young man asked, winking his eye at my mother.

"No, man, nothing for you," Dolores said.

There were three of them who came over to us. They were the same three young men who had been playing music at the juke-box.

"Can you tell me the time, please, Miss?" the same young man asked my mother, who lifted her nose high and looked in the other direction.

"You've got a watch," Dolores said.

"Where are you going?" another of the young men asked Dolores.

"To Town," she answered.

"Oh? We're going to Town too," the man replied.

My mother rolled her eyes and sighed.

"What's the matter with your friend?" the man asked Dolores.

"She's not feeling well," Dolores said.

"Then I can make her feel better," the man said.

Just then the bus came. It was a "Whites Downstairs, Non-Whites Upstairs" bus.

Poor Dolores was quite out of breath by the time we got upstairs. The young men said that Dolores must sit downstairs with me as she shouldn't climb stairs in her condition. She said that she would prefer to sit downstairs but that the white "gaartjie" didn't look like a friendly man and would probably chase her upstairs with all the other coloured people.

The friendly young man then asked the conductor himself, but he was told that he didn't make the laws and that laws were laws, besides, some white people might complain and he could lose his job.

"I'm just doing my job!" he added.

Dolores said that they must not worry. She was well pregnant, but not crippled.

The young men sat upstairs with us and teased my mother all the time. She pretended to ignore them by looking out of the window, but I could see the glint in her eyes and the smile dancing at the corners of her mouth. Every so often she would clear her throat. Dolores, on the other hand, answered all their cheeky questions, and the young men thought that she was my mother.

We nearly missed our bus stop. It was I who nudged Dolores and said, "Mustn't we get off here?"

"Yes!" she said, jumping up.

"Hold the bus, driver," the young men shouted as we all scrambled to our feet. I was so scared that the bus would ride off that I was the first one down the stairs, followed by my mother. Dolores was about to get off when the impatient conductor pressed the bell prematurely, and the driver began to pull away as Dolores reached her foot out to step onto the pavement.

"Hold it, driver!" the young men shouted behind Dolores, but it was too late to stop the bus from jerking forward.

It was a badly-timed jolt which sent Dolores sprawling onto the pavement.

The white conductor looked at us without expression and rang the bell. The young men jumped off the bus as it pulled away.

"Is she all right?" they asked my mother, who was trying to get Dolores to her feet.

A crowd had gathered around us. Some people we knew, some we didn't.

"If it was a white woman," someone muttered, "It would have been a different case."

Dolores sat wincing and holding her back. She squeezed her eyes tightly shut.

"We'll help you get her home," the one young man said to my mother.

He and his friends helped Dolores to her feet and just about carried her up the hill to the house.

"And now?" Ma asked, as the men carried her in.

"Dolores fell off the bus," I said eagerly.

"Make them tea," Dolores said to my mother. "There's some tennis biscuits in the cupboard. Ouch, my back hurts."

"First see to her," the one young man said. "Don't worry about us."

They made themselves comfortable in the sitting room.

Ma told me to call Nurse to come and see if Dolores was all right.

"First to see the lights go on!" Radia shouted as I ran across the road.

CHAPTER 33

Nurse said that Dolores should be all right, but that we must watch her.

My mother sat in the lounge speaking to the young men and Ma sat at the kitchen table with her ear against the radio, listening to a play, while watching the meat for Sunday lunch.

I washed myself, put on my pyjamas and climbed into bed. I was exhausted, not physically, but emotionally, and fell asleep almost immediately.

When I woke in the morning, I knew instinctively that something was amiss. It was Cedric who told me.

"Dolores is in the hospital," he said.

My heart froze.

"Is she going to die?" I asked him.

"No, man," he answered irritably. "She's having the baby sooner than she should – that's all!"

"Oh," I said, as if I understood.

I went to church, but I might as well have stayed at home because my mind wasn't there.

Before lunch I dried the dishes for Ma while she listened to *The Bell Tower* with a cup of tea.

We ate our lunch in silence.

"It's terrible without Dolores," I said, breaking the ice.

"Yes," Cedric answered, stirring his cold jelly into his hot custard and making a real mess.

"I wonder if she's okay," Ma said.

" I phoned the hospital," my mother answered, "but there's nothing doing yet."

"I wonder if we can visit her?" Cedric said.

"Maybe we can take a walk up after we've cleaned the kitchen," my mother suggested.

"I'm telling you," Ma said most authoritatively, "they don't allow any visitors before the baby is born."

"Ons kan sien, Antie Lenie," Cedric persisted.

"You can ask Nurse if you don't believe me," Ma argued.

"Then leave it maar," Cedric said irritably.

"I think we must rinse the baby's nappies for her," my mother said. "You can't put new nappies on a new baby. The child can get nappy rash."

My mother soaked the baby's nappies in the new baby bath while I packed all the baby clothes out of the drawers and back again. It was so exciting to think that a little human being could fit into these tiny things. Everything was so pretty in lemon and white.

There was a knock on the door. We all rushed to get it – my mother, Cedric and myself.

Ralph, one of the young men who had helped us on the bus with Dolores, stood there, all spruced up, with a bunch of sweetpeas and box of Black Magic chocolates.

"She's in the hospital," my mother said, fumbling with her hair.

"But these are for *you*!" the young man said.

I could see my mother blush as she led the young man into the sitting room. She took the flowers from him and told him to sit down.

"Love is in the air!" Cedric said as he placed the sweetpeas in a jug of water.

"Oh, go play!" my mother said, giving him a playful tap with her foot. She asked the young man to excuse her and went into the bedroom to emerge later, all dolled up and smelling like a rose garden. She sat down opposite the young man.

Cedric called me to the back.

"They want to be alone a little," he said, "You help me make the tea."

"If you help me hang the nappies on the line!" I answered.

CHAPTER 34

The little baby boy lived for a day and then died. His little lungs were just too weak to cope with breathing outside of his mother's womb. Dolores was shattered. She sank into an oblivious depression and cried all the time.

My mother took the day off work and went to the offices of Safmarine to ask if they could contact Uncle Reg and get him to come home as soon as possible.

I felt very sorry for Dolores and sat with her while she cried.

Uncle Reg, when he came back, was more angry than he was sad. For once, Dolores kept out of his way. He kept asking her questions, over and over again the same questions, and each time she fumbled and mumbled and cried. There were no relevant answers to his irrelevant questions. Even Ma told him to stop it.

"You people don't understand!" he roared. "My son is dead! Someone has to be responsible! Why was she in Wynberg? Why take a bus in her condition? Is it asking her too much to stay at home where she is safe?"

"Ag, Reggie, she didn't know she was going to fall off the bus. You act as if she did it on purpose," my mother said.

"'Ag, Reggie,' you say!" he roared. "Then why did she have to sit upstairs? Why?"

"It was a 'Whites Downstairs, Non-Whites Upstairs' bus," Ralph said. Ralph was becoming a frequent visitor.

"What?" Uncle Reggie screamed. "Surely she could sit downstairs? She could have asked the conductor! Anyone could mos see that she was pregnant!"

"We did, Uncle Reg," I said. "We all wanted to sit downstairs, but the conductor said we couldn't."

"He was only doing his job, Reggie," Ralph said.

"Doing his job?" Uncle Reggie shouted. "Doing his job? That is why coloured people are what they are – just coloured people. Because of people like you. You accept inhumane treatment and say he is only doing his job. My little boy is dead and he didn't even have a chance!" Uncle Reggie buried his head in his hands and sobbed like a heartbroken child. Ralph got up and went to stand on the stoep.

"Go to your room, Reggie," Ma said.

"Los hom, hy's hartseer, Auntie Lenie," Cedric said.

The little baby didn't look dead. He was pink and perfectly formed, lying there in his little white coffin as if peacefully asleep. He was very, very tiny. Dolores had dressed him in a beautiful white nightdress, she fidgeted with his sleeves and hair as if expecting him to wake up soon. She wasn't sad any more, but she wasn't her bubbly self either. She looked as if she had aged somehow, and as if the light had gone out in her soul.

The funeral was very quick and impersonal. It was conducted in the church vestry and there wasn't even a hymn. The baby's name was Allan Reginald Paulse. After the funeral, Uncle Reggie seemed to be somewhat calmer. Dolores told him about Uncle Herbie.

"I didn't even go to the funeral," she said.

"Yes," Uncle Reggie said, "Uncle Herbie was a old man. He had his days."

"Did he really?" Dolores said. "Did he really? He wasn't happy, he died an angry and defeated man."

"I am angry, too," Uncle Reggie said, "but I will not be defeated!'

"What can you do, Reggie?" Ma said. "You can't do anything. Look what they did to Braam Fisher – and that was a white man. You'll end up in jail."

"I will leave the country!" Uncle Reggie said solemnly. "I will not rear my children in a country where they are second-grade citizens. Nowhere else in the world do you find this kind of situation."

"Reggie, Reggie," Ma said nervously, "where will you get

the money? Do you know how much it costs and what about work? What will you do? You can't go to sea and leave Dolores alone in a strange country!"

"I have money," Uncle Reggie said, "the money I was saving to buy a car – and I won't leave her alone. I'll do any work – even sweeping the streets – as long as it's an honest living."

"Reggie, Reggie," Ma said, shaking her head, "you live in a fool's paradise."

Uncle Reggie was quiet for a while. He lit a cigarette and drew on it.

"Do you know," he said in a calmer voice. "Every time our ship pulls into port, I have to remind myself that I am coloured. I have to read the signs before I get on a bus or a train, before I sit on a bench on the station."

He drew on his cigarette again. "I've had enough of it and believe me, it won't get any better. I'm leaving."

CHAPTER 35

Uncle Reg and Dolores applied to emigrate to Canada.

There were mixed feelings about this in the house. Ma said that they would stay there for a week and then be right back here.

"It's too cold there with all the snow that falls and doesn't melt until the summertime."

"Don't talk nonsense," Uncle Reg said.

"In any case, there's central heating," Dolores added.

She seemed to be satisfied, if not excited, to emigrate from the land of her birth. Each time we challenged her about it, she would sing chirpily:

"I love him, I love him, I love him, and where he goes I'll follow…"

She told me that when I grew up and fell in love, I should remember her, and then I would understand how she felt.

The thing is, I didn't think I would ever fall in love with a boy. Even less so could I ever see myself kissing a boy! The thought of it made me want to run and hide. I'd sooner be a nun!

Ralph had become a regular visitor. He was there almost every evening. He seemed to be genuinely fond of my mother, but Dolores said he would never marry her because his family would never accept me.

"Why?" I asked, flabbergasted.

"Because, Darling, just like me, you are illegitimate. Men don't marry women who have illegitimate children."

What an ugly word. It was almost like, "You are coloured…"

I felt a lesser person than I ever did before.

And I was angry.

It was easy to cover my arms beneath my jersey and

pretend that the colouredness was not there, but how could I hide the fact that I didn't have a father from myself?

I became cold towards Ralph. I wanted to challenge him, to hurt him, but I knew I couldn't really since I only had what Dolores had said to go by.

Ma pestered my mother about Ralph too.

"What's on his mind?" she'd ask. "Did you meet his parents? What about Kathy?"

"Haai, Mummy," my mother would say.

Ma would reply: "I'm getting old. I won't be here forever!"

CHAPTER 36

A strange man came to see Uncle Reg, who wasn't home yet. Dolores told him to sit down and made him a cup of tea.

The man was nervous and fidgety. He kept asking how long Uncle Reg would be. Eventually he said he could wait no longer and rose to leave.

"Can we give him a message?" Dolores asked. "Can he phone you? Can we tell him your name?"

"No, no," the man said. "It isn't serious. Actually, I wanted him to take something to my brother in Canada when he leaves. It's nothing really – just fishpaste, middle cut and biltong."

Just then Uncle Reg came in. The man started blurting out his request.

"Sit down, sit down," Uncle Reg said. "I'll get us a drink, then we can talk."

The man seemed to enjoy drinking and soon lost his nervousness and urgency.

He told Uncle Reg that his brother was living in self-imposed exile in Canada. He told Uncle Reg some horrific "secrets" which he didn't want us to hear, but as the alcohol loosened his tongue, so it impaired his sense of hearing and we could overhear everything.

He said that a civil war was inevitable.

"I'm not prepared to wait and see it happen," Uncle Reg said. "And I'm not prepared to lose my life or rear my children here – not in this country!"

"Some people are," the man mused. "Some people are."

He said that the nation would have to come to its knees before anyone would make a concerted effort to right the wrongs that had been committed in the country.

"… If there *is* a way to put things straight," he said. "And unfortunately, we will suffer as a nation – black and white together – side by side. Maybe then we will turn to each other."

Ma sat herself down on the settee, eager to join the conversation.

"Things look a lot less hopeless for us now that the Progressive Party is the official opposition. At least we have some voice now – indirect though it may be!" she said.

"It's not enough," the man said. "Apartheid must be abolished altogether. It is a crime against humanity."

He gave his empty glass to Uncle Reg and watched him pour the brandy into it. He held his hand up to say "When!" when Uncle Reg had poured the required amount of Coca Cola into his glass.

"True democracy demands equal rights," he said firmly. "Equal opportunities – one nation – from the people for the people."

"It will come," Ma said. "It has to come. Maybe not in my lifetime, or that of my children, but maybe their children's children will live in a better South Africa."

Uncle Reg looked at Ma, horrified. "And you're prepared to live and die here, knowing that you will never be a real South African?"

"I was born here," Ma said simply. "What is the sense of running away?"

"We're not running away," Dolores said. "We want to start a family overseas."

Ma wasn't listening. Nostalgically, proudly, she was relating to this strange man the story of her grandfather who had been a French prisoner of war many years ago. He had jumped ship at Simonstown and had taken refuge with a coloured family. He later married one of their daughters.

"Most of their children married whites and went to live in Rhodesia. My mother married a coloured man from Simonstown."

"It just goes to show," Dolores said. "There can be coloured blood in a lot of white people."

"They don't want to know it," the man said, and told of similar circumstances in his own family.

The man was crying real tears and singing "We Shall Overcome" in a slurred voice.

Eventually he fell asleep on the settee and we left him there and all retired to bed. Cedric told us that he woke in the middle of the night and left, just like that.

CHAPTER 37

Radia and I had made a habit of spending Saturday afternoons together. Since we went to different schools, we saw so little of each other during the week. Sometimes we would go to bioscope or we'd take a walk into Town to look at all the things in the shop windows. At other times, especially in the cold weather, we would buy Abbassie's polonies, which we would eat warm with atjar at home.

One day we were walking past the City Hall when we saw some boys walking towards us.

"Shall we cross the road?" I asked Radia.

"No," she said.

"But they're white," I said.

"So?" she asked.

As the boys came closer to us I noticed that one of them became fidgety. He started lagging behind the others, then stopped to tie his shoe lace, deliberately turning his back towards us.

"He's blushing," Radia whispered.

Something about this boy seemed so familiar – the way he bent his head – a lot like Uncle Reg. We might have passed unnoticed if his friends hadn't called to him:

"Hey, Christopher! What's taking you so long?"

Radia and I passed the boy just as he looked up in response to his name.

Blushing profusely, he quickly looked away from us.

"I'm coming!" he called to his friends, who were leaning against the pole on the corner.

"But that's your cousin, Christopher!" Radia said in dismay.

"I know," I said, too shocked to say anything else.

"But he must have recognised you," Radia continued.

"I don't know," I said.

"Come, let's go after him – just to embarrass him," Radia suggested.

"No, leave him," I said. " He's white now. Don't embarrass him."

"Then you are white and I'm white too," she said indignantly, "if *he's* white!"

"Radia," I said, "Calm down!"

"He could at least have greeted us. We used to play together – I used to like him and Fadiel used to say he was his best friend."

"Calm down!" I said, even though my heart was racing, as if I had been running fast.

"He didn't have to say anything," Radia continued. "He could have nodded his head – that's all."

"True," I answered.

"My word!" Radia said, echoing her mother's favourite two words, "Do you mean to tell me when you turn white you have to turn your back on your friends and relatives?"

"I suppose you have to," I said, remembering the times we had spent playing 'Blind man's Bluff' and even the times they had teased me and made me cry. It had left a big gap when they had stopped coming to us for lunch on Sundays.

Radia continued ranting on about him being white, saying that everyone in her family could be white too, since they all had lighter skins than Christopher.

"I wonder if they are happy," I said.

"My Oemie's mother was a Jewess," Radia said.

I stopped walking and she stopped a pace ahead of me.

"And now?" she said.

I smiled at her and she sighed.

"What?" she asked.

"You can all be white if you want to," I said, "As long as you don't walk past me in the road pretending not to know me!"

"Oh, go!" she said, and gave me a playful shove.

We walked on in silence for a while.

"It just makes me so cross," she said afterwards, adding:

"To think I used to like him when I was small."

CHAPTER 38

Ralph and Uncle Reg had become quite friendly with each other.

"You look after my sister when I'm gone," Uncle Reg would tell him every so often.

The day Uncle Reg and Dolores left was here before we were ready to accept what was happening.

Dolores made me promise her that I would continue to look in at Aunty Sal at least once a month. She made me promise to write to her, just as she would write to me. She gave me her crystal necklace to remember her by and I gave her my one cent coin.

We sat around all morning trying to make light of their parting, but each one of us had a lump in our throats.

Ma kept complaining about her arthritis.

Cedric said that he didn't want to move back into the back room so my mother said that she and I would take the room for ourselves.

Friends of Uncle Reg called all morning to wish him and Dolores well. He told them all the same thing: "You must make up your minds to come over. Things will never get better here."

Strangely, each one agreed with him and felt they would emigrate, but not just yet.

Eventually it was time for us to go to the docks to see them off. Ma said that she would have to watch the ship from the stoep because her arthritis was too sore to walk around in the docks.

Uncle Reg held her face in his hands and said: "I'm sending for you as soon as I'm settled!"

"This is where I gave birth to my children and reared them, this is where I will die," Ma said defiantly.

"You have to face it, Mommy," Uncle Reg argued. "After District Six, they are going to move you out too, and then what are you going to do? Live in Bonteheuwel away from everything?"

"Over my dead body," Ma said. "Over my dead body!"

"Mommy, Mommy," Uncle Reg said, and kissed her.

"Go!" Ma said. "Go now, before the boat sails without you."

There were more friends of Uncle Reg in the docks. We all sat around in the lounge of the ship sipping cold-drinks.

The *HMS Pendennis Castle* was a beautiful ship and had a festive atmosphere on board. I went ashore to stand back and admire her.

A layer of cloud like a tuft of cotton-wool sat on the mountain. It was an otherwise clear day for the first week in July. The small fishing vessels bobbed gently on the water and some opportunistic seagulls squawked about overhead waiting for someone to drop a morsel.

The dull ship's horn penetrated the chill of the day. People – non-passengers – came spilling out of the ship, down the gangplank, and gathered on the quay.

Some people wore dark glasses to hide their tears. Others threw coloured rolls of streamers to their friends on the quay, who caught them and held on until the distance broke the streamers as the ship moved away.

Dolores's eyes met mine and she waved. She was so happy, so satisfied, like a little child.

The water churned beneath the ship as she moved away from the quay. The crowd cheered and the passengers waved their handkerchiefs about frantically.

A strange emotion came over me as I stood there watching the tug lead the ship out of the harbour into the great open ocean. It grew smaller and slowly smaller as it neared the horizon. It wasn't sadness that I felt, or emptiness. It wasn't loneliness or longing. It wasn't anger or envy. Maybe it was a sense of defeat.

The people on the ship were not distinguishable any more. They were mere dots on a match-box bobbing on the water.

CHAPTER 39

The crowd at the quayside dwindled until only we were standing there. The ship was now a dot on the horizon, the tug safely back in the harbour.

"Let's go and buy milkshakes on the Parade," Ralph said, taking my mother's hand in one hand and mine in the other. We walked together to his car in silence.

Absent-mindedly, I kicked at a stone, which sent a group of seagulls scattering and squawking. A little one remained. It was much smaller than the others, almost like a dove, and pure white. It looked me in the eye and then took off. It soared above the cranes and then disappeared into the afternoon shadows. Ralph and my mother saw it too. Their heads moved in unison as they followed its flight.

"Beautiful!" Ralph said.

We walked up towards Town. The City Hall stood majestic, steadfast as an anchor overlooking the Parade, with Table Mountain in all her splendour behind her.

My mother and Ralph were walking ahead of me, holding hands like two children. They stopped at the statue on the Parade and looked back at me.

Ralph smiled as they waited for me to catch up with them. He bent down and whispered in my ear.

"I didn't hear you," I said.

He dropped my mother's hand and took me aside, dropping to his haunches. He took both my hands in his and looked into my eyes.

"What would you say," he said, "if I asked your mother to marry me?"

I was stunned. I looked at my mother sitting on the steps of the statue, with all the pigeons gathering around her questioningly.

She looked happy and at peace.

"What did she say?" I asked, turning to face Ralph again, a warm glow washing over me.

"I didn't ask her yet," he said. "I first wanted to know how you would feel."

"I'm very happy," I said, hugging him. "But don't leave the country, and don't make me go too."

"We won't leave," he said, "things will change here."

"What are you two talking about?" my mother asked, coming over to us.

"I was just telling Kathy that things will change for the better in this country," Ralph said.

"They must change," my mother added.

Ralph winked at me.

"Why don't you ask her?" I prompted him. "Go on, ask her!"

"What is going on?" my mother asked inquisitively.

"Nothing's going on," Ralph said. "I was just telling Kathy that I wanted to go and look at rings in Town."

My mother frowned and said, "Oh!"

"Ask her, Ralph," I said, nudging him.

"Bertha, will you go and look at rings with me?" he said eventually.

I narrowed my eyes and looked at Ralph again.

"… At engagement rings and wedding rings and then will you marry me?" he blurted out in one breath.

My mother grabbed Ralph and hugged him tight.

"Will you?" Ralph asked again.

"Without question!" my mother answered.

"I'll walk home," I said.

"Come with us," Ralph said.

"No," I said, "I'm big enough now. And I don't want to be derde mannetjie!"

They laughed.

"I'm old enough, you know," I said, "and I understand."

CHAPTER 40

I walked up Hanover Street. Beyond the shops the area looked like a haunted war zone. Here and there a house, once part of a terraced row, now stood vulnerable without its neighbours because its occupants had not found other homes – or were they perhaps waiting for some change of heart at the eleventh hour? A few children played happily in the rubble among the ruins with a dog.

Further on the wind whined through the ruins behind St Mark's church. In the distance the bulldozers droned, systematically crunching through the concrete and sending dust swirling into the wind. I carried on up the hill.

Absent-mindedly, I wandered into Motjie Ismail's shop. Baai looked somehow older today, his eyes looked tired.

"So your Uncle Reggie's gone, hey, Gogga?" he said.

"Yes, Baai," I said.

"You know, Sweetheart," Baai said slowly, "It looks like we may all have to move sooner or later."

I did not expect to hear that from Baai, but I guess he just wanted to speak his heart because he wasn't even looking at me any more.

"… Soon there will be no-one left any more. No-one to come to the shop … no reason to get up early on a Sunday to make koeksisters … no business …"

"Maybe things will come right," I said to Baai, hoping that I could cheer him up.

"No, Sweetheart," he said, "Things won't come right for us – more and more of our people are leaving the country. Dullah even has applied to go to Australia."

Just then Radia came into the shop.

"I've got something to tell you," she said excitedly as she picked out a pound of potatoes for her mother.

I wondered if Radia's mother was going to have another baby.

"Let's go!" she said, beckoning me to follow her out of the shop.

"Can you keep a secret?" Radia asked excitedly, and grabbed my little finger to toss in for secrets.

She told me that she really liked a boy who lived in the next street down from us and that Fadiel said the boy liked her too.

"I've got a secret to tell you too," I said to Radia, once she had told me how much in love she was.

"You too?" she asked, surprised.

"Not what you think," I said quickly, and offered her my pinkie to toss in again.

"It's about my mother and Ralph," I said.